# Randy is Miranda A Gender Transformation Caper

Penny Flowers

Published by Clumsy Cantos Co, 2023.

RANDY IS MIRANDA A GENDER TRANSFORMATION CAPER

**First edition. May 27, 2023.**

Copyright © 2023 Penny Flowers.

ISBN: 979-8223038368

Written by Penny Flowers.

# Table of Contents

# Punching the Clock

"What is the hold up? We've got to clock in."

"What's your best guess, Randy?"

"Parker's hitting on someone?"

"Bingo."

This was a typical morning conversation. We all hated it. Our shift at Pack-It Industries arranging gift baskets for the D&H company was starting. It's an okay job once you get into it, but our boss made punching the clock extra stressful.

"That bastard. He does it just to fuck us all over," I said to Cheryl who was in line ahead of me.

"It's the truth but he's the boss," she shrugged. "What can you do?"

The truth was there's nothing we could do. The warehouse still had an old-fashioned punch clock. Parker, the site supervisor, held the day's time cards in his grip. No one gets on the clock until 5 minutes before the hour. And if we're not clocked in by 5 minutes after the hour we get docked 15 minutes from our checks. It shouldn't take more than a few minutes for everyone to get in the door but Parker likes to slow it down.

He holds back the time cards of certain women and won't punch them in until he's messed with them. Anything from comments about their appearance to lewd double entendres. He usually ignores me because I'm the only guy in my department. Today I was the last one in line. If he didn't stop harassing the women ahead of me I was going to be fighting for my 15 minutes.

I stepped out of the line so I could see him at the desk. Sure enough he was holding Annie's card over his head forcing her to lean across the desk to take it. Leaning so that his face was practically buried in her big chest. Gross.

I could see Annie fuming. She finally grabbed the card from him and forced herself to smile. She whispered something in his ear before the next person stepped up. Parker leered.

"Seven o'clock," he called after her.

Ugh, I thought. So that rumor was true. Annie was his latest target. She was playing along even though she clearly wasn't into it. Parker had ways of getting his favorites to see him after work. People will do crazy things to keep their jobs.

A lot of us only needed this job until the new semester started. Mostly we're young and single. The big bosses think high turnover reduces costs so they hire a lot of part-time students. The ones that Parker really pressured were the full-timers who didn't have college waiting. They had families to support. I guess it's a devil's bargain.

"We've barely got two minutes," said Cheryl.

Parker saw me looking in his direction and glared at me. I stepped back to my spot against the wall. The line started to move quicker but not fast enough. Finally, I was through the door and standing in front of Parker's table next to the time clock.

"It's nine oh six, Randy. You know what that means."

"Seriously? You saw me in line 5 minutes ago."

"I saw you dawdling back there. I didn't see you in front of me at 9:05."

"No way. You can't do this."

"Are you going to fight about it? I've got your card here. I can hold on to it until you lose a half hour."

"What do you want from me?"

"I want you to go to your station. Start packing pralines in raffia and get out of my sight." He flicked my card at me and waited to see what I would do. I let it go. Just one more week and I'd have saved my expenses for the next semester. So long, Parker. No more overpriced chocolate pretzels in wicker baskets.

I should have been able to quit right then and there but there had been a little setback in my budget. I had my summer budget planned down to the last penny. It didn't factor in the dent I put in my apartment wall. A week before I was swinging free weights around, trying to get back in the routine. I had music on. I shouldn't have started dancing with a fifteen pound dumbbell. Hello triceps, goodbye security deposit. Losing a quarter-hour from my check wasn't doomsday but it still stung.

I tried to let it go while I worked. Soon I was absorbed in arranging fancy crackers and confections in baskets for customers. I had a line of them ready to be wrapped in cellophane and boxed for shipping. Doris walked by my station. She was in charge of apples and pears.

"Parker wants you to stop by his office on your lunch break," she said.

"For real? What now?"

"I don't know. Don't piss him off or we'll all pay the price. D&H big wigs might do a surprise inspection this week. He's been in a mood."

I tried to guess what he wanted. Of course it had to be on my time, not the company's time. Maybe he needed my address at school to mail my tax stuff. This shop did nothing digitally. Paper time cards, paper inventory sheets, paper checks handed out in paper envelopes every Friday. Pack-It wouldn't spend any money upgrading operations on the shop floor. Pretty ironic since D&H does all its sales online and they are practically our only client. The Darryl and Hazel gift company didn't want to deal with the mechanics of assembling its own product. They contracted the warehouse. Parker reported to a boss higher up at the downtown Pack-It office but it was the D&H VPs he had to please. At lunchtime I grabbed a handful of complimentary toffee popcorn and headed to Parker's office. It wasn't a big space but he had managed to fit in a couch and mini fridge along with his steel desk. I didn't want to think about what went on on the couch.

"You wanted to see me sir?"

He didn't ask me to sit down. I stood there waiting for him to look up. The concrete walls were bare except for a poster taped above the mini fridge. It was an ancient pinup of a TV actress in a swimsuit. I wondered if it was Parker's or had been hanging there when the company moved in. The blow-dried hair and poky nipple pushing through the red bathing suit probably turned him on. He had his tie knot loosened and his top button unbuttoned. You'd think he had put in a full day's work already. Finally he looked up at me.

"I walked through your department twice yesterday and a couple of times last week. You weren't at your station any of those times."

"I was probably helping on the loading dock. Was there something you needed?"

"I need you to be at your station packing baskets."

"I'm keeping up with my baskets. More than quota. You can check my reports."

"I don't care about your paperwork. If you're here you should be stuffing baskets. You're not paid to work the trucks. You're a packer, not a receiver. For all I know you could have been in the washroom jerking off. Working around all that pussy must get you hard, huh?"

That was not anything I wanted to talk to him about.

"I'm just here to work, sir," I said.

"I'm docking you an hour for each time you abandoned your station."

"You can't do that. I put in a full day's work."

"I'm not convinced. You're a half day short by my count. If you want to go home and cry about it, we can call this your last day. The payroll will look better without you."

I saw he had a couple of big ledgers open on the desk. Was he trying to balance the books by cheating me out of time?

"I need my days," I insisted, "I've got four shifts next week then I'm out of here. I've got expenses."

"Boo hoo. Everyone in the shop has expenses but nobody wants to put out."

"I'm good at my job. Have you got something against me?"

"What do you want me to say? I don't like the way you look. That's reason enough."

I wanted to kick in the steel frame of his stupid desk. Who did he think he was? I stood there and argued, defending my work ethic, while Parker rolled his eyes and berated me. He was clearly entertained by my frustration. He wouldn't budge on the docked time.

"Get out of my office," he said when he was tired of me. "Keep acting like a shit and you won't get paid for this week at all. If you're lucky I'll let you punch in on Wednesday."

I stormed out of there fuming and muttering under my breath.

"We'll see who punches who."

# Miranda Rites

When my shift was done I texted my best friend Louise. I couldn't bear to go home and fume by myself. She told me to come straight over. I found her waiting for me with cold drinks and sympathy. While I told her about my shitty day she rubbed my shoulders.

"I always help the guys on the dock," I told her. "It keeps things moving. He didn't care. You know what he said? 'Stop helping people.'"

"A true asshole," said Louise, working a knot out just below the right side of my neck. "Should we pay my cousin from New Jersey to kill him or something?"

"Would he?"

"Probably not. Scratch that then."

"A hitman isn't in my budget anyway."

"And he pulls this shit with everyone?"

"Yup. He gets a bonus for cutting costs. Instead of incentivizing us to innovate and find efficiencies, he writes people up and dings their hours. That's not even the worst of it. He tries to make the hot ones earn their time back with favors."

"What kind of favors?"

"Just the kind of favors you would expect."

"That's disgusting. Why doesn't someone report him?"

"His targets don't start anything for fear of losing their jobs. Plus someone higher up would have to care. The Pack-It bigwigs don't even come around the shop."

"It just isn't right." Louise was working down the muscles of my spine. It was pretty nice except her nails dug into me the more she heard about Parker.

"Ease up there. I've had enough abuse today."

"Sorry." She sat next to me and held my hand.

"I get why some of them do it. If I could get him off my case for a quick blowjob I might consider it. Too bad I'm not a chick."

Louise let my hand go. She had her game face on and I could guess what she was thinking. She was dressing me up in her head.

We've done cosplay together since we met at the anime club in high school. I used to play as a vampire hunter or a warlock. From the beginning she was trying to talk me into trying female characters.

"What's his type?" she asked. Before I could answer she was up and looking in one of her closets. She's hauled out a bin of costume pieces.

"I know what you're thinking and you can just stop. He likes a skinny ass, big tits. Too much makeup. Pretty much describes the women he hires."

The warehouse had a good mix of people overall. But all the white women were a certain type. Parker's type. I was the only guy who did baskets. In spite of good complaining, he wanted a guy on hand to load up the dollies at the end of each shift. The women were willing and capable but Parker thought of that as a guy's job. That's how I got in. He didn't want the ladies to crack a nail piling boxes. But being a guy must have made me a competitor. To him women were prey.

"I don't know how you stay in a place like that," said Louise. "It's so 20th century."

"This is the last summer. Next year I'll have my degree and find a desk job to suffocate in for the rest of my life. But I'll be suffocating with a 401K you know? Besides, the pay at Pack-It is okay when Parker doesn't fuck me over."

"What if you got someone else to suck his dick to get your hours back?"

"No one there would do that for me. I wouldn't let them. And I don't hear you volunteering."

"True that. Not even as a favor for my best friend."

Louise never talked about chasing after guys for sex. She wasn't shy about making lewd comments but she had no desire to hook up with randos. For blowjobs or anything else. She didn't seem to be attracted to girls and she talked about cute guys sometimes, but neither of us really put any energy into dating.

Louise held up a blue dress like Dorothy wore in The Wizard of Oz.

"Do you think he'd go for you in this?"

"I think he'd be more into a slutty scarecrow type. I can't picture Annie alone with him. The mayor of Munchkinland would be sexier than Parker."

"If you could fix it for her, you would. But people are funny. She might get angry at you if you stepped in and spoke up."

"It's her decision I guess. What blows is I don't even get the choice to turn him down. Just because I don't have tits."

"I think you'd actually do him if it paid for that hole in your wall."

"It's not an option. I'm sorry I said it."

"No you're not," Louise teased. "You're wondering what it would be like."

"Stop it." I got up off of her couch. I couldn't imagine it. I wouldn't. Walking into Parker's office, two guys that didn't like each other. Checking each other out. Asking if he wanted his cock sucked. No. Not even for the money. Not even as a fantasy. Louise held a prom dress on a hanger in front of me. I pushed her arm away.

"Please stop."

"All right. No gay for pay. What's plan B? Sell your scooter?"

"Sell something. I dunno. Maybe I could donate plasma. You got any tequila left?"

"Tequila? Oh my God, that's it." Louise was darting from foot to foot like a bird.

# RANDY IS MIRANDA A GENDER TRANSFORMATION CAPER

"What's it?"

"You can't go down on your boss but Miranda could."

I busted out laughing. Miranda was a big joke between us.

"No. Miranda is not making a comeback."

Miranda was a character we made up. Last summer we had gone through a half a bottle of tequila while planning cosplays for an anime convention. Louise kept asking what it would take for me to wear a dress. I told her there was no way I would do it. Then I had the drunk crazy thought that if my character was a spy, and a master of disguise, I might dress as a woman to catch the villain.

Louise of course had the perfect costumes, and I was drunk enough to go along with it. She dressed as a French jewel thief, complete with a penciled mustache, striped shirt and a beret. She looked like a mime. Drunk me squeezed into a black maid's outfit with goth Lolita frills and a blue wig. After more tequila I was chasing her around her apartment to recover the jewels. When I finally cornered her I said "These are your Mirandas. You have the right to remain silent. Anything you say will be used against you."

That's when she blurted out "Oh, Miranda. I don't want to be silent." We both fell over laughing. You had to be there.

Ever since then she's been asking when Miranda is going to come back. The answer is never. Drag is cool, but not my thing. I don't even think about cosplay much if I'm not at Louise's. Not since I've been working full-time and trying to read ahead for next semester.

Now Louise was begging for the return of Miranda. I went to her cupboard looking for that bottle of golden liquor. She called after me.

"C'mon. If you did it, you could be undercover for real. Wear a wire and get him to say you have to have sex to get paid."

"Miranda would never pass," I said.

"Yes she would. I'll make you look really hot. For real. Padded bra, sexy outfit, makeup."

I came back into the room brandishing tequila and limes.

"And then what?"

"Get him all hot. When he unzips his pants, pull off the wig and bust him."

"I'm a man, baby," I said in my best Austin Powers voice.

"He'll have to pay you. Plus extra for hush money."

"That would be awesome but still a big nope."

For the next three shots we argued this strategy. She thought I could go to Parker and pretend to be my own sister pleading to make things right. She didn't convince me. Eventually I put down my wedge of lime and told her I should go. We had one of our awkward moments that happens when we're drunk. It's like we each wait for the other to say something unsaid. It's either leave or cross a line we're afraid of.

"Thanks for listening," I said. I kissed her on the cheek. She patted me on the ass as I turned away.

"Be safe," she called after me.

# Sunrise before dawn

Walking toward home I imagined Parker thinking I was a hot chick looking out for her brother. Batting my eyelashes. Whispering innuendo. Except somehow I got it turned around in my drunken head. Instead of me offering to go down on him, I was imagining Parker reaching under my dress and into my panties. Finding my cock. Oh God, he'd put me in the hospital. There could be no good outcome. Unless he found something smoother there. Snug cotton riding up into feminine folds. A groove he could slip a finger into while I earned my pay. If I were a real woman, the further I let him go, the more proof I would have in a harassment suit. God. Where did I get my mind? I couldn't get these images out of my head.

At the end of the next block was a small club. Every time the door opened to let somebody in or out there was a blast of throbbing bass and flashing lights. It distracted me from my mixed up thoughts about sex with my nemesis.

The door opened again and the two who stepped outside were a sight. Two flamboyant women with short dresses and high heels. They were walking my way, laughing and leaning into each other. Their red and blue sequined outfits were a little fancy for a neighborhood place. Their makeup was heavy with eyeshadow colors to match their outfits. When they got close I could see glitter in their lip gloss. I wondered if they were performers or just loved attention.

"Better hurry hun," said the one in red. "It's almost last-call."

Why would they think I was headed there? I'm not a club person and I certainly wasn't dressed for it. I was still wearing my work clothes. A rumpled button-down with the shirt tails hanging out over my boring khakis. I don't know who they thought I was. Just drunk and friendly I guess.

"Oh, I'm just headed home," I said.

"You should go in for a drink. It's trap house night," said the one with blue sequins, slurring a little.

"The DJ is on fire!" said the red one. They stood close. It was friendly, not threatening, but I couldn't get past without walking around them.

"It sounds like fun, but I'm all out of drinking money."

"Aw, you poor thing. That's just not right."

"Angela, buy this lad a drink."

"Marsha, we're on our way home. You promised."

Marsha, the one in red, looked at her friend Angela and crossed her arms.

"I remember when you didn't have money for a drink." She turned to me and added. "How quickly they forget."

"Fine, then. Twist my arm. I'll do it." Angela touched my shoulder. "You're going to be our guest. What's your name?"

My mind was flying trying to figure out how to extricate myself from this situation without being rude. It had already been too long of a day. I did not need to be adopted by total strangers and taken to a dive bar. That's when it hit me. These women weren't what they seemed. The tequila filters fell from my eyes and I saw that Angela and Marsha were guys. OK, that's not correct. I guess it's misgendering to say they were men. I didn't know if they were trans or cross dressers, or drag queens, or if I even understood the difference. I just stood there staring.

"Excuse me, is there something on my face? Did my lashes come loose? Marsha?"

"I'm sorry," I said, "I'm already a little drunk. My name is Randy. You look great. Both of you do."

"Thank you," said Angela. She hooked my arm in hers. "Come get a little more drunk with us. I'm buying."

Marsha took my other arm. Both of them had sleek, slender arms. I noticed their hands were delicate. Angela had long elegant fingers made even longer by her curling fashion nails. Now I wasn't sure why I had gotten a guy vibe. I had been swept up by two sexy women. Louise would never believe it. They led me down the block, ushering me inside. Strobe lights were flashing. I took in the space a little bit at a time. Things were clearly winding down. There was a small group at the end of the bar. One person was dancing by themself in front of the DJ booth. Over the noise of the electronic music, the bartender hailed my new friends.

"Back so soon? You know it's last-call. What are you having? Make it quick."

"Tequila?" I said, a little unsure of myself.

"Three tequila sunrises, Marvin. Unless Randy doesn't want a girly drink."

"It's all good," I said. I was being discreet but I kept watching the two of them to see how they moved. The way they stood was femme. The way they held their arms. Their voices were low but had a lilt. There were little glimpses in the jaw and shoulders that they might not be who they seemed but as we talked those uncanny flashes went away. I was having a drink with fabulous club girls.

They peppered me with questions. Before I knew it, I was telling them all about my day. Including Louise's idea about going undercover as Miranda.

"Absolutely not," said Angela.

"What kind of a world is it where a person needs to buy their way out of a bad situation with sex?" tsk'd Marsha.

"There's no justice, is there?" said Angela.

"Not really," I had to agree. "In any case I would never pass."

"You don't need to pass Randy. You just need to be who you are. That's how things work out."

"Always be yourself, isn't that what we say Angela?"

Angela sipped her drink, eyeing me over the rim of her glass. The red and orange of the cocktail swirled like fire.

"He can't stop thinking about it."

"We should take you to the Soma Swap."

The sweet grenadine was making me fuzzy. Or maybe it was the trance beat on the speakers. They couldn't be thinking I would go with them to another bar.

"What's the Soma Shop?"

"Swap, not Shop. At Halsted and Clark? You must have seen it."

"The resale store?"

Angela looked at Marsha. "He doesn't know."

"It's a swap shop."

"You're talking about that place with the pink tricycle in the window? They sell used junk and vintage clothes."

"Oh, no no no. They sure don't."

"Nah. They make your junk disappear and turn you into Cinderella."

"I think you ladies are weird. You can't mean what I think you're saying."

"It's on the down low," Marsha stage whispered in my ear. Her breath was warm. I wondered if she was coming on to me. I got my answer when her hand brushed my crotch.

"Soma fixes everything," she said. I pushed her arm away.

"Manners," said Angela.

Marsha put her hands back where I could see them. I emptied my cocktail glass. I was feeling ok. All those shots I did with Louise had made a nice soft bed for the sunrise to land on. Marsha and Angela were nice. And so very pretty. But not my type, whatever my type was. Did I even know? Louise would get a kick out of them. For me though, home felt like the place to be.

"Ladies, I need to be on my way. Thank you for the drink."

Angela smiled a broad toothy smile.

"See how you feel in the morning and then thank me."

"I'll be fine," I said, sliding out of my chair and holding the table for balance.

"Yes you will!" said Marsha.

# Same bed, different body

The first thing I did when I woke up the next morning was roll over and pull the covers over my head. Daytime needed a dimmer switch. I peeked out of my blankets through half closed lids. The sun coming through the blinds hinted at a beautiful day out there. I tried to decide if that created any obligation on my part. It was Tuesday, no work until Wednesday since I had Saturday shifts.

I took a quick inventory. No headache. No stomach woozies. I felt a little weird, but not hangover weird. I didn't need to pee which is what usually gets me out of bed. I could lie here as long as I wanted and not think about money or bosses or foil wrapped pears.

Not only didn't I have a hangover, I felt extra well rested. The linen sheets were cozy on my legs. The weight of the blankets was like a warm hug. I considered jerking off. Memories of Angela and Marsha came back. They were certainly sexy, whatever their identity. But not my fantasy. My mind wandered to Louise.

We liked to snuggle. I had been *yes, no, maybe* about taking it further for so long that I hardly thought about it anymore. Our friendship mattered more, plus I wasn't aroused around Louise. Well that's not entirely true. There were twinges, but I always pushed them aside as too risky. Why complicate things?

I hugged a pillow. Sometimes I got a boner for her when we did cosplays. She wasn't shy about stripping down to her underwear in front of me when she switched between characters. I'd watch her until I caught myself getting aroused then I'd look away. I used to wonder if she felt it too, but we were both too awkward to act.

# RANDY IS MIRANDA A GENDER TRANSFORMATION CAPER

We usually flopped down on the couch after a few drinks. Her head on my shoulder. We've been like that since we lived on the same dorm floor. Our crew of geeks and nerds used to gather on the floor in a big cuddle puddle made out of pillows and plush and each other. It got casual touchy but not too sexual. Louise and I always shared the hugs and light touching even when the others weren't around. Lately it had been a habit. We snuggled, but it just seemed ordinary.

On the other hand, active cosplay with Louise could get pretty rambunctious. Whether it was dancing, or play fights between characters, it was always over-acted. The first time it got openly sexy was the night we invented Miranda. I grilled her about the stolen jewels. She was defiant. I remember my hairy arms in ruffled sleeves, wrapped around her. I had her pinned. My stockinged legs pressing hers against a wall. We were nose to nose and her mouth was so close. We went from acting foolish to fooling around.

I knew she could feel my cock pressing against her. "What are you hiding under that apron?" she wanted to know. She whispered dirty suggestions in fake French. My interrogation got more physical. Her fingers tugged at the bowed knot behind me. Poking and tickling turned into groping and kissing. We fell onto the couch and with great passion, and promptly passed out together.

I have a groggy memory of Louise's hand under my skirts before dawn. I remember her bra was very white in the dark room. Her hand felt good on my sex. I tried to tell her this, but I fell back into a drunken sleep. When I woke up she was still out, wearing the striped shirt again. So maybe I dreamed the whole thing.

These memories weren't making me horny, just confused. I rolled over in bed. Something was under me. Did I leave my clothes wadded up on the mattress when I fell asleep? I swept an arm under me to push them away and caught hold of myself. There were no clothes. I could feel my hand on my chest, but my fingers were feeling something soft and cushy. They sank into my flesh. I pushed the covers aside in a start.

The oversized t-shirt that I wore to bed was sitting all wrong. I pulled it up to my neck while sitting up. A pair of big round breasts dropped out. They hung over my ribs defying my eyes. I couldn't believe what I saw.

This was no mere swelling. I saw fully formed, almost pendulous breasts that curved up to support nipples that were clearly not my nipples. Mine were small flat discs with a patch of hair between. These were thick and long surrounded by wide areolas and not a hair in sight. I could feel the weight of them. My balance was different. I had to adjust my posture to hold them up while my mind raced. They had to be fake. Was this a crazy costume I fell asleep in? I felt behind my neck to see if there was a strap or zipper. Nothing. But my hair was longer. I tugged to make sure it was mine. It was.

I needed a mirror. Standing up, my t-shirt dropped back into place, but the breasts beneath filled it out. I made it to the bathroom. The face I saw in the mirror was a stranger's. The jaw line was different. There was no morning stubble. I was looking at a woman. In a panic I pushed the waistband of my pajama pants down. Usually they drop right off, but I had to slide them over my hips which were much too wide. My heart raced. Beneath the pubic hair I saw nothing. My penis was gone. Where my balls had been I felt folds of skin that parted when I touched. The stranger staring back at me from the mirror was fully female as far as parts went.

I had insane thoughts. Maybe I was someone else who just thought they were me, Randy. But that was crazy. If I wasn't Randy, I wouldn't wake up thinking about Louise. But how could I be in someone else's body? Let alone one that kind of looked like me. There was a resemblance to me like a sister or cousin would have. This was my room. Was my real body in a stranger's room somewhere? That made no sense.

I remembered coming straight home from the bar. The two women. They must have drugged my drink. Some combination of hypnosis and hallucination was making me think my body had been switched. That Soma stuff they talked about must have planted the suggestion.

All the while I was thinking, my hands were moving over my torso. They ran the contours of this strange, but well put together, form. The hips were wide, the backside round, the belly flat. The breasts, though full, were a good size for this frame. I saw that the legs were toned but still had my covering of hair. That talk about a body swap shop had to be a gag. They couldn't really have any of that Soma. I refused to believe it existed. But the illusion was complete.

I didn't know how I could come to my senses. I wanted to run out of there and find those two, but where would I look? The only clue I had was the location of the shop they talked about. I knew the storefront, it was near a busy intersection. Maybe someone there could explain what's going on. My mind was racing.

This had to be reversible. Best case scenario it would wear off soon. Otherwise I needed to find answers. Coffee couldn't hurt. And maybe a shower would help chase away whatever was in my system. Keep active and keep the panic away. That was the first step.

I started a pot of coffee then headed back to the bathroom. Standing naked on the cool tiles I allowed myself a minute to appreciate what I had become. I had never wished for anything like this, but it wasn't horrible. Not like Dr Jekyll and Mr Hyde. It felt like me in a way that wasn't me. It felt good to breathe. I felt healthy. The body responded to my movements gracefully, not a bad fit. I even understood that I was kind of pretty.

If those women had been on this Soma, it didn't affect them like it affected me. Angela and Marsha were women but had little tells that made me question their gender. In this body I could pass. The hairy legs were a little irksome. It was a silly thought to have because I was sure I would get my own legs back. They would look weird hairless. I grabbed my razor and took it into the shower with me anyway.

I let the water run cold hoping it would snap me out of a dream. It was a shock, but it didn't change me back. The feeling on my nipples was like an alarm going off. I backed away from the cold spray. The sensation of them standing firm was like nothing I had ever felt. My hands covered them automatically. They were too sensitive to the cold. I adjusted the faucet and let it run down my back until it was warmer. I squeezed some body wash onto a cloth. It felt good to touch the skin I was in. Water and soap ran down me. I lingered at those responsive nipples until I was distracted by the feel of the shower flowing over the area between my legs. I was going to have to explore. How could I not? I touched myself where my penis had been. I felt the shape of the slightly protruding lips, and the short hair over them. They separated at my touch. I knew where this could lead and the more I allowed my fingers to examine, the more determined I was to go further. I found things where they ought to be. Outer and inner and hood and clitoris. Each felt unique and responded to attention. I began to rub.

I turned so the water wasn't in my face. One arm cradled my breasts while the other stroked at the nub of clit beneath its thick hood. It was just as sensitive as the underside of my cock head, but there was more to it than that. Warmth spread through my whole lower regions. The lips begin to swell as blood flowed to the region. The inner folds opened more and more to the press of my digits. Soon I was pressing my palm against the hard nub while my fingertips were slipping lower. Soon I had a finger inside myself. This was nothing like tugging at myself under the covers with my rough hand. I felt this with my whole body. Not just the wet vaginal excitement or the straining nipples. The pleasure ran up and down my spine. I could feel it was going to be intense if I made myself come.

I didn't want to fall and have a concussion in the shower on top of being in a woman's body. I switched the water to fill the tub and settled on to my back. In no time I was breathing hard. The pleasure of my fingertip on the small hole of my vagina as it slipped past, and the small pull of suction as it slipped out, compelled me to stroke deeper. My other hand was on the clitoris. I rubbed the looser flesh of the hood back and forth over the firm nub within, stroking then squeezing.

"This is what a woman feels," I said aloud. My voice was higher, but husky with heat. My hips began to roll, splashing water. I pushed my feet against the tub bracing myself as a series of little peaks began to build into a wave. I was making sounds. My whole butt lifted out of the warm bath water. My shoulders leaned into the back of the tub as walls inside of me began to tremble and spasm. The big wave came over me and although my head was above the water I was drowning in ecstasy.

In the orgasm all sound and color was muted. There was only intense pleasure and release chasing through my changed body. I don't know if I screamed but as I caught my breath the sound of the running water filled my ears. I turned off the tap with my foot and sank down into the warmth up to my chin. My breasts floated a little.

This was not hypnosis. No trick of perception or suggestion could have felt like that. I was a living, breathing woman. I picked up the razor from the tub caddy and began grooming my legs like it was the most natural thing in the world.

# Soma

In order to confront reality, which is to say the outside world, I pulled on a pair of my skinny sweatpants. They hugged my curves but I got them on over my boxers which felt a little ridiculous. What I needed were some panties or even some tighty whities. I wasted more time than I should have checking to see if the lines on my legs were good. I obviously had no bra, so I found my loosest t-shirt. It had a gym logo. Something I got as a freebie one time when Louise and I had decided to get fit. The trainer at the free session said that in time I would fill it out. I think he meant with biceps not boobs.

I didn't look bad. Some women are so vibrant and attractive they make the simplest outfits look good. This was that kind of body. Was I being vain? Posing in front of the mirror I knew I would turn heads. My full hips and slender shoulders brought the outfit to life. I tousled my nearly dry hair and sighed. I might never have figured out my type, but I definitely didn't go for assertively sexy types who showed off their curves. And they didn't spare any attention towards me either. I wondered if I would get unwanted attention when I was out looking for answers. Probably.

For the first time that day I thought of Parker. If I walked into his office like this, he would be all over me. It was like a wish was granted. The crazy talk about seducing him to get my hours back was now a possibility. This weirdness couldn't be connected to Parker. In stories, wishes always backfire. Something would go wrong. Probably everything. Plus, did I really want to use my time in this body confronting my least favorite person? I clung to the idea that this wasn't permanent.

I needed Louise's advice. She could help me through this. She would kill me for not calling her immediately, but she was at work. If I texted, she would think I was pranking her. A selfie would prove it, but that would literally be TMI. She needed to see it in person to believe it. I would have to wait until we could meet.

What would she do if we were together now? She'd do the smart thing. Research. I got out my laptop. Searching for Soma brought up all kinds of references to old novels and eastern religious stuff that were dead ends. I searched for gender change and brought up articles on hormone therapies and surgeries. That was too conventional. This was an overnight miracle.

Finally I found mention of an experimental, fast acting pill in a pharmaceutical journal. The language was beyond me. It was much too technical, but I copied the chemical name and combined that with the word Soma in a search window. Finally I got a lead.

The blog of a biochemist in Singapore mentioned the drug with references to banned research and secret work groups. The translation wasn't that good, but there was a quote from a Swedish journalist speculating on the massive profits coming if human trial results were good. I followed the Swedish lead and finally got something worthwhile.

Promising variants of the gender changing drug were in production for use in clinics but pressure from the American FDA was holding it up. Despite this a black market for it was thriving in Berlin. Even more interesting was gossip about it being a club drug in Atlanta and Miami. This had to be it. I tried to remember if either Marsha or Angela had a southern accent. Sort of. Anyway I was the living proof that Soma had made its way North.

I needed to find the local connection and get them to switch me back. I grabbed my keys and wallet and discovered I couldn't squeeze anything into my pockets. What does a woman do? I didn't have a purse. I found a canvas tote bag from an anime convention and threw in my phone and essentials. I was dressed and ready to go.

The bag made me think of Louise's cosplay trunk. I decided to text her. How would I explain it all, though? There was one thing that would sum it all up. I tapped in MIRANDA IS ON THE CASE. That would get her attention. I added a couple of heart emojis and hit send.

# Street walking

It was a cloudless summer day. The sun on my cheeks felt nice, but it wasn't so warm that a walk would get me all sweaty. The Soma neighborhood wasn't far from my place. I hoped I could walk down the street without being noticed. Just another pretty face. It wasn't my face that got attention.

A couple of biker-looking dudes sitting outside of a sidewalk café stopped their chess game and tracked me as I walked past. I could feel their eyes on my backside until I dodged in front of a dog walker. The dog seemed curious. It kept yipping and sniffing at my heels until the dog owner snatched it up and told me "I think he likes you."

I nodded and picked up my pace. At the next crosswalk the light was red. A stranger got too close and looked me up and down.

"It's a beautiful day," he said.

"Yes," I replied, trying not to make eye contact.

"We could make it more beautiful," he whispered.

I crossed in the other direction to get away from him. A young guy paying for parking at a kiosk was staring as I approached. He wet his lips. When he saw me notice, he looked embarrassed. His panicky brown eyes were kind of pretty. I might have missed a step. We both looked away. I was surprised by his vulnerability. For a moment I felt appreciated. I didn't know how I felt about that, so I didn't let myself look back at him as I hurried along.

I've been on my own in the city for a few years. I always felt anonymous and secure on the sidewalks of familiar neighborhoods. I could walk and be alone with my thoughts. This felt like having a spotlight trained on me as I crossed an enormous stage.

"Sweet!" I heard from a voice across the street. Two jocks were at a bus stop.

"Oh, yeah." The second one waved. Ugh. *Just pretend you're invisible*, I told myself.

Finally I saw the shop ahead of me.

It was the same used and consignment store that had always been there. The hand-painted Soma Swap sign above the door might have been new. I remembered the store but never noticed the name. I recognized the vintage tricycle in the display window. Behind the tricycle was a mirror with gold decals on the glass. In fancy letters across the top it said Portal To Your Dreams.

Nothing suggested that this was anything but a retail store. There were price tags on everything in the window. Inside the space was small and the stock was limited. There were clothes on circular racks. There was a bookcase with only a few books and some trinkets for sale. Tables were covered with everything from hardware and toys to cameras and shoes in no particular order. There was a changing area to one side and an open door leading to another room at the back. That door had a velvet rope hooked across it, barring access.

I wanted to just walk back there and look around, but there was a clerk. They sat next to a glass case full of costume jewelry reading. There was no register and they weren't paying me any attention.

"Excuse me," I said. "Has this place always been called Soma?"

They looked up without closing their book. The clerk was a skinny boy with dyed black hair that was slicked back on one side and fell over in long bangs on the other side. He wore a little bit of eyeliner.

"I don't know, I'm new here."

"But, is Soma something you sell?"

"Just what you see on display."

"Oh, you see, well maybe they were making it up, but there were these two women Marsha and Angela. They, uh, said you had Soma here."

"I don't know what that is."

"But you work here. It's the name of the shop."

"It's just a name."

"It was something else. I came here hoping to find out about it."

I wanted them to ask me about it so I could explain my predicament. But they looked back down at their book.

I stepped away from the display case and began picking things up off the tables without looking at them. There had to be an answer here otherwise I didn't know what to do.

"Is there more in the back?"

"That's employees only," they said without looking up.

No one else was around. How much room did a place like this need? The front of the shop was barely making use of the space, the back must be used for something else. Maybe I could poke my head in. I started browsing in that direction. On the wall by a garment rack I got a glimpse of myself in a mirror. My first thought was surprise that someone else was in the shop. My second thought was that she was letting it all hang out. Only then did I realize it was me.

The breasts under my t-shirt were obviously braless. I suddenly felt immodest. Maybe there was something here I could use to contain them. If I had to walk home without getting any new information, at least I could reduce my chances of being harassed. There was some lingerie on the rack and something that looked like a corset. That would hold me in, but I didn't know if I could figure it out. There were some tube shaped tops there too. I picked one up and held it in front of me. How would I even know the size? And on top of that how would I pay for anything? I was broke thanks to the Parker problem. I stood there holding the clothes, helpless.

"You look a little confused. Can I answer any questions?"

I turned to see a man in a white smock wearing thick glasses. He was balding on top, the rest of his head was trimmed to the same length as his thin beard. He looked like a fuzzy but friendly kiwi fruit. I looked at the clothes in my hand.

"I've never done this before," I said.

"That was my guess. My name is Michael. I work here."

I knew immediately he didn't mean he sold second hand clothes and knick-knacks.

"Are you the Soma guy?" I asked with an air of desperation.

"I don't know you," he said. A note of caution crept into his helpful expression.

"My name's Randy, uh Miranda. Marsha and Angela sent me. Sort of."

At their names, the caution turned to annoyance. Whatever they were to him, I was afraid it would turn out bad for me. But he gave me a sympathetic look. Maybe he knew better than to lump me in with those two characters. He took the garment from me and set it on the table.

"We should probably go in the back."

Michael took me by the arm. His grip was just firm enough to let me know it wasn't entirely my choice. At the same time, he nodded approvingly at me. He unhooked the velvet barrier and let me go.

In the back room there were a few bins of odds and ends set beside a bench for tagging and selling. It was a production set up not too different from what we had for D&H at the Pack-it warehouse, just smaller. Michael took me past the inventory, behind a dividing screen. There on a table was a machine I didn't recognize. Rows of glass canisters, filled with white powder, were on a shelf. A bowl was overflowing with empty pill capsules. They were red. There were plastic bags of other colors under the shelf.

"What color capsule did they give you? Wait, let me guess." Michael studied my face and looked me up and down. "Stable, very stable. Must have been this red. They know that's off limits. It hasn't finished trials."

"Wait a minute. They didn't give me anything. They bought me a drink. I don't even know them." I had already guessed they had slipped me something, but seeing this set up confirmed it. This was an illegal lab. Or at least a processing outfit for making pills.

I was angry. Anger felt different in this body. It usually hits me like a stomach upset. Mild nausea and twisting my innards to hold it back. Now I was boiling hot. My fists were clenching. I was sure my face was red. And I was aware my nipples were stiff enough to be pointing at this stranger. I crossed my arms across my chest, a move I must have seen women do a thousand times and never paid attention to. It was a defensive posture, although Michael seemed more interested in my face than my breasts.

"I can see they've made a mess of things. Although the results are superb. When did this happen?" He ran his hand over his bald head as if it would organize his thoughts. I could practically see the gears turning. It looked like I was going to get some answers.

"Just last night. Close to two in the morning."

"You better have a seat." He pointed to a couple of chairs at a desk behind the pill-maker. "First thing you probably want to know is, it should wear off in two to three days."

"Days? Can't you reverse it? I have work tomorrow."

"I'm sorry Miranda, if you had gone through proper channels you would have been briefed on this. But that's the time frame. Unless you get pregnant."

"What?"

"You don't have a bun in the oven do you?" The fuzzy man actually chuckled at that.

"No! I haven't even..." I couldn't say it. What did he think I was?

"They spiked my drink."

"Oh goodness, I'm going to cut them off." He opened a desk drawer and pulled out a file folder and a little fishbowl thing full of square packages. "You better grab a handful of these, just in case."

He was offering me condoms.

"What is it you think I'm going to do with those?"

"Well there's a lot of reasons Soma is popular. It's always disappearing out of this outpost. Not all our sample population cares that much about sex. But whatever motivates our subjects, sometimes they get unexpected urges." He thumbed through some papers. "I'm going to ask you to look over and sign some documents and waivers."

"Waivers? Do you not get that I didn't ask for this? In fact this setup can't be legal."

"We are in what you might call a gray zone. We're quite professional, follow all the protocols. Here, this one describes chemistry and all reported health events. It's all within acceptable safety ranges but we will want you to report any discomforts."

"Actually, I feel fine." I was surprised to hear myself say it, but Michael had a calming personality. I was sitting with my legs crossed, admiring my long fingers as I took the stapled pages from him. I was comfortable. That was not a common feeling for me.

"Why the storefront? What do Marsha and Angela have to do with you?"

"The FDA is timid. Even though the public wants this research done. Marsha and Angela were indispensable while starting our American trials, even if they went rogue sometimes. You wouldn't believe the hoops we had to jump through to get INTERPOL to leave them alone." Michael leaned in to let me know he was sharing secrets. "They had an ecstacy distribution network that suited our purposes. They know everybody. We're trying to be a little more conventional now."

"That's great for you, but I can't go to work like this."

"Can't you take a couple of days off?"

"I can't afford to." I slumped back in my chair. My reality wouldn't go away despite the bizarre situation I was in.

Michael's eyebrows went up.

"Oh, we haven't gotten to the money part. You know that in test trials subjects are compensated." He pulled out another paper, this one a single sheet. "You just need to sign the waiver and I can disperse $1500 today in cash."

"Wait, what? $1500?" That was a lifesaving amount of money. The thought of it pushed away the craziness of the day for a moment.

"I'm sorry it can't be more," said Michael. "There are bigger stipends if you enroll in a longer term trial."

My shock and anger at suddenly being a woman were melting. It was unexpected but temporary. It was an incredible story to share with Louise. And, the feel of my body now that the fear was gone, was invigorating. My mind flashed back to my time in the tub.

"What's in the waiver?" I asked.

"It says that you are responsible for your own actions while using Soma. It says that you won't give blood during the change. It also says that the Soma organization will provide medical coverage during the year following your participation. Except for voluntary pregnancy. We really advise against that. Plus you won't change back if that happens. If you don't have questions, I can get the cash box while you read it over."

I didn't have any questions because I was already going through the dense paragraphs of type. It was all as he said, just with a lot more legal jargon. Not like anything a mob drug ring would have, I thought. That was reassuring. When Michael came back I had one question.

"It's two days, you said?"

"More likely three. Sometimes people re-assert early. But you look so naturally at ease, I think you'll get the full experience."

With the money, another day didn't matter. I could just quit my job. I picked up the pen and signed.

# Dress up

The merchandise on display at the front of the store took on a different light now that I had a stack of hundred dollar bills in my bag. Michael had walked me back to the display where he first approached me.

"William can help fit you," he said. "They'll know your size. They have quite an eye for fashion." He waved to the clerk then disappeared into the back room.

To live this for a couple of days I would need some underwear that fit my shape. And at least one outfit that would let me blend in. Blend in where? That was the question. I had to find Louise and shock the hell out of her, but after that?

I couldn't let go of the idea of showing up at work just to blow Parker's mind if not his dick. If I was stuck this way why not fuck with him? The timing was right. If I went there today, it would be before payroll was filed. If I got my hours back, it would be a bonus on top of the Soma money. If I didn't, it would still be a kick. Without the financial stress, the whole thing seemed kind of funny.

"Hey William," I said. "I need some day wear, but I also need something kind of slutty."

William put down their book and carefully placed a bookmark before getting up. It made me wonder about their purpose here. Not customer service, certainly. They walked right past me and started pulling items from different racks. They seemed to know what they were looking for and never gave me a second look.

"Over here," William said when they had an armload of items. We went into a dressing room. It was big enough for two even with a bench to one side and a rolling rack full of hangers on the other. A wicker basket at the end of the bench was filled with packets of hand sanitizer and wet wipes, but also more condoms.

This place was really pushing safe sex. What went on in this dressing room? I had, in fact, thrown a few condoms in my bag on Michael's insistence. I could present one as "Miranda" to distract Parker if it got to that point. While he was fumbling I could start recording on my phone. It was a crazy idea, to let it go that far. But still....

While I schemed, William was looking me up and down.

"The sweats have to go of course, but I think we can keep the shirt. Do you mind if I cut it?"

I shook my head. William produced a pair of scissors from their back pocket. I wondered if they used them to play with their haircut when the shop was empty.

"Hands over your head," they said, putting two fingers on their jaw line while I raised my arms. After a moment of consideration William took a handful of the shirt and pulled it taut. The scissors flew as they trimmed around me, cutting most of it off. He worked high above the boob line, barely an inch below my nipples.

"Lower," they said.

With my arms down, the shirt tented over my breasts and hardly covered them. Any horny guy who saw them would be hypnotized wondering what they would see with my arms up. I had to know myself. Putting my hands behind my head was all it took to flash the lower slope of my curves.

"Nice work," I said.

"We're not finished, take it off." William sighed. They couldn't have looked more bored. I wanted to slap them. Was that tone just a ploy to get me naked in here, or was it supposed to make me less self conscious? Maybe they were only into guys. I pulled the shirt off and gave it to them. The air on my flesh was prickly. I did the cross armed thing again but that only lifted my chest toward William.

They were too busy snipping away at the shirt to pay my boobs any attention. In a minute they were done. When I put the top back on there were holes cut across the front, artfully teasing a view of my cleavage. It was a distressed style I had seen in magazines. William knew what they were doing.

"Can I compliment you now, or is there more?"

"No, that works." They slipped the scissors back in their pocket. "I'd offer to do your hair but then I'd have to sweep up."

"No, that's fine. I don't know what a new haircut would look like when I change back."

William didn't blink at that. I guess we were done pretending they didn't know what Soma was. From the bunch of clothes they had gathered William handed me a pair of panties. They were virginal white with a scalloped trim. There were also sheer leggings and a black skirt to go over those. The long macramé vest he chose would cover up my scandalous t-shirt. There was an ordinary blouse and stretchy sports bra too, that I could change into when I was done begging for attention. I held the underwear.

"I guess I should ask you to turn around."

"If you want," they said without actually moving. I had to consider what I wanted. William was here to assist me, but I was about to drop my pants.

"You know I'm a guy, right?" I said.

"Well that's a matter of perspective. Do you actually feel like a guy or are you clinging to who you remember being yesterday?"

Ugh, I thought. Are they a philosophy major or something?

"I'm not used to whatever this is. But I'm still me."

"Yes, the slutty version of you. I believe that's what you asked for."

"There's something I need to do that will be easier if I look trashy. Do you think I can pull that off?"

"Do you need to practice?" They looked at me like I had shown up at class unprepared. "You haven't tried anything out yet, have you?"

The words felt like an accusation. William looked annoyed, as if I was incompetent.

"I found out some stuff in the tub," I said and blushed. "Look, I don't intend to screw this guy, I just need to get his attention. Do you think I'll pass?"

They actually gave it some thought. I guess they had given up the idea of rushing back to their book.

"Did they know you as a guy?" William asked.

"Yeah."

"Well, don't fall into your usual way of being around them. If your habits assert themselves it will fight the Soma. They'll see the old you in your body language. Are you going to let them touch you?"

"Maybe?" My mind fell back into the drunk thoughts I had the night before of Parker reaching into my pants. The further I let it go, the less able he could deny a harassment charge. He'd be suspicious if I just showed up and asked him to undress.

"You'll know what to do. Unless you were particularly repressed as a guy. You're not a virgin are you?"

"No," I huffed. It wasn't a lie. But it was a small and awkward set of experiences a couple of years before I even knew Louise.

"The way you're put together a guy is going to start here." They cupped my breast. "Am I right?"

"Yeah. That's pretty clear." Now that I was getting used to his manner, William wasn't so bad. Direct more than judgmental. And their hand was on my boob. I surprised myself by taking their other hand to my chest.

"How is it for you?" I asked.

"You know," they shrugged. "I'm on the clock."

That made me think of Parker, but only for a second. William started kneading my breasts, more of an examination than feeling me up. It felt surprisingly good. Their hands slid over my nipples, catching each finger against the tips. The feeling as they stiffened spread, sending an alert through my upper body. My lower parts responded with a wave of warm desire. William slid a hand down over my waist to caress my butt. I pressed into them. Through my sweats and their jeans I felt a firm shape. My hands pressed against their back, pulling them tight.

Right at that moment I thought of Louise. What would I tell her about this impossible encounter, rubbing up against another man's penis in a booth? I shared everything with her. How could I justify what I was about to do?

"Do you want to stop? Your natural responses seem fine," said William. "I don't think you'll have any trouble fooling your frenemy."

"He's no kind of friend. He's truly evil. But I don't want to think about him right now."

I didn't want to stop what we were doing. The feel of their body aroused me in ways I couldn't relate to from my limited experience.

"This isn't what I expected," I said. "I didn't know it would feel like this."

"Don't assume it feels the same for all women," William said. Their hand fell from my butt. They were right of course. I didn't imagine Louise or any of the women I knew found themselves hooking up with strangers in shops. But I was aroused and William seemed willing. I knew I could go home and take care of those feelings in the tub. That wasn't the real thing though.

"You're right," I said. "But this is my one chance to....To Go All The Way," I laughed. Louise would understand that. It was like anime logic. Like something in a pop song. And William wasn't unattractive in their way. They were skinny and affected and not all together nice. But I liked the way they felt. I wanted to know what they would do with me. When they gently tipped my chin up to kiss me, I began to find out.

I felt stubble on my cheek when they went for my ear lobe. I smelled spice on their neck. I kissed them there. Our limbs entwined and I clung to William for balance. At the back of their neck I enjoyed the bristly feel of their hairline where it was razor cut. I ran my fingers through the longer hair that was so carefully shaped.

"Bodies are amazing," they whispered. "Male and female share the same space, live the same lives, even think the same thoughts. But you'll never feel like this as a man."

William hooked their fingers in the elastic hem of my sweats and slid them over my hips dropping to their knees as they went down. Their face was in front of my wispy pubic curls where William inhaled deeply. I wondered if I smelled fresh. They twirled some hair between their fingers.

"I could do some shaping and styling here. But not until you're satisfied that everything works as you want."

They tapped one of my knees. I lifted my foot out of the rumpled sweats. I held their shoulder for balance as I kicked the pants away with the other foot. When Willam stood, they lifted the newly designed shirt over my head and tossed it on top of the other items. I stood before him completely naked.

William faced me in a dyed black dress shirt and skinny legged tight black jeans. They were wearing more makeup than I was. I'd never worn any at all except at Louise's insistence and only then under protest. But I saw how it brought out William's character. The black eyeliner suited them. Their stylish look highlighted my nudity; I felt exposed.

"Bodies," they repeated and smiled. It was a friendly look that betrayed just enough desire to let me know what was about to happen would not be a chore for them. They began undoing the buttons at their collar. I decided to help by exploring what lay behind their jeans. I unhooked the buckle of their belt. The snap and zipper of the jeans opened easily to reveal a black bikini style brief. It was as sheer and delicate as you could get and still be called menswear.

If William's emo style could be described as androgynous, the bulge in their underwear was anything but. It was decidedly male and the shape of it could be seen under the fabric. I couldn't help comparing the length of it to the modest endowment that had abandoned me overnight.

I wasn't bothered by the difference. The heat in my body grew. I was intrigued by the horizontal ridge that extended to the seam. There was something irregular about it. I ran my hand over the shape. There were bumps where there shouldn't have been. William smiled.

"Feel free to check it out," they said.

I knelt down and peeled back the fabric. I was face to face with a length of flesh that had been studded with steel posts and round closures. I had seen pictures of genital piercings before. Strange internet photos of rings through the tip that looked painful and anything but erotic. This was different. The bars ran like a ladder of chrome from the base to the head of their penis. It was exotic.

"Are you going to ask me if it hurt?" William chuckled.

"I'll assume it did. It's pretty cool." I took them in my hand. My fingers fit between the metal work. William began to stiffen. I realized that in my position I'd be expected to do something with my mouth. My body was responding, but I wasn't here for William. They were supposed to be helping me with my new feelings. I stood up.

"You lead," I said demurely.

William finished undressing. They folded their clothes neatly on the bench, stroking themself a time or two in the process. All very businesslike. They had composure. I admired the compact curve of their skinny butt, the wiry muscles of their arms, the tiny nipples, one of which was also pierced. Even comparing male to male they were very different from me. In my current form I was suffused with attraction. I wanted to press them to my curves.

When they returned their attention to me, their member was up. I had plenty of experience with that and knew what I could do to them. But there were other instincts at play. I reached between my legs and felt my wetness. I took some and began to massage William with it. Their hand reached between my thighs and cupped my lips. We stroked each other until I noticed a bead of pre-cum on the tip of their erection. William had two fingers in my wetness. It seemed that we were ready for penetration.

"People who come here for some Soma," I said between short breaths. "They just do it right here? That's what the basket of condoms is for?"

"We let people express themselves. It's in our mission statement."

"And you can put a condom on, right over the piercings?"

William pulled a condom from the little wicker basket. They tore the corner of the package with their teeth then began to roll it down over the studs as I watched.

I wasn't sure how to navigate the difference between our heights. I wasn't going to get on the bare floor where unknown numbers of people had walked. I let William turn me around to face the bench.

"Put a hand on the wall and put one foot up," they said.

I did as he asked and felt their sex slide along the groove of my buttocks as they leaned over me. They put a hand around my waist. With the other William fondled my dangling breasts, making them sway as William's palm wove between around and over them.

I was losing myself in their touch when their cock slipped down and under me. The head rode over my clitoris before backing up to my slick opening. This was it. Nevermind the pronouns, a man was entering me. It was like nothing I had ever experienced. Feeling just the tip slip in gave me shivers. Both of Williams' hands were on my hips and I pushed mine against the wall for balance. I felt each metallic bump press my lips, as they slowly penetrated me with their full length.

I was wet enough that there was little resistance. Instinctively I squeezed around them to heighten my sensation. Their low moan let me know they liked it too.

"I'll go slowly at first," they whispered in my ear as they reversed their stroke. Again each bump ratcheted past my opening, drumming pleasure through me. They started a slow rhythm that I tried to match, pushing back against them. I wanted to turn around and look at them but the angle wasn't right. I reached back and put one hand over theirs. William hesitated for a second not knowing what I was signaling.

"Just keep doing what you're doing," I said.

William fucked me, gradually picking up the pace of the movement. I squeezed their hand, welcoming the thrusts. I reared back to meet them, thrilling to the impact. I felt my pleasure reaching for a peak. Then William was going full throttle, chasing their own release. I had to keep both hands on the wall for balance.

I was so close I began to make little cries. I pressed my cheek against the wall and let the rest of my weight press down against the person inside me. They reached around and rubbed my clit fast. They knew what they were doing. In seconds I would be coming. It filled my body like nothing I could ever have dreamed. The sounds I made were loud. I thought of Michael in the back room, but I didn't care. The whole world could hear and I wouldn't mind. I was a woman and there was a man inside me. And I was right there.

"Please, please," I cried. "Don't stop." But they did stop, for a fraction of a second, just long enough for me to teeter on the edge. Then they were at me again, pumping frantically, and I began to spasm with pleasure. I shook and moaned, and suddenly I needed them to stop, but they were right there with me, taking their finishing strokes and groaning like a bull.

William went slack, falling against me and wrapping their arms around my belly. We were both panting. My knees felt weak. Slowly William withdrew. We both settled on the bench.

"And that's how that goes," they said.

Then we were silent. William's hand was on top of mine now. Wetness puddled under me. I understood why there were wipes in the wicker basket.

"Thank you," I said when my breathing had returned to normal. "I can't imagine sex being like that all the time. As a woman I mean."

William, ever detached, answered.

## RANDY IS MIRANDA A GENDER TRANSFORMATION CAPER

"Not everyone has good sex, I guess."
"Then I'm glad you're good at what you do."
"Thank you. What did you say your name was."
I gave a little exasperated huff then laughed.
"You can call me Miranda."

# Loving Louise

We were tidying up the dressing room with cleaning wipes when I remembered that Louise only had a half shift that day. She would be home a little after 2:00. If I called a ride I could get there before she did. Thank you, Soma money. I didn't have to pinch pennies so I opened a rideshare app and called her address up. As a bonus I wouldn't have to parade myself on the sidewalks in William's designer slut-ware.

The driver was a woman. I caught her sneaking glances at me in the rearview mirror. It was a cold look. Yesterday we both would have ignored each other, but I knew my looks set her off. It's not like I chose the body I was in. And who was she to judge my outfit? I didn't judge the generic polyester polo shirt she was wearing. She would look fine in it if she wasn't stuck driving around in her car all day.

I felt the stress weighing on her. Work makes people see everyone as a rival. She probably assumed everyone is either beneath her or trying to be better than her. I wanted to say something nice to let her know I wasn't like that. I couldn't think of anything, so I just watched the blocks go by.

When we were close to Louise's, I realized we were going to pass the bar where this all started. If they were open, I had enough time to poke my head in.

"Can you let me out early?" I asked the driver. "The next light works."

"Anywhere you want," she answered tensely, like she couldn't wait to be rid of me.

"Thanks. Sorry for the short ride but I'll leave a tip."

"Sure you will," she said.

After I got out, I added a tip that was more than the fare. Maybe she'd remember me when she saw it and be kinder to the next floozy looking woman who got in her car.

In the daylight I could see the sign above the club door. It was called Mirror Mirror. Inside the house lights were on, filling all the corners that were just shadows the night before. There was no music and no one at the bar. A big guy in a white T-shirt was wiping down tables.

"The bartender's not in yet," he said. "So I can't get you a drink."

"That's okay. I wasn't looking for that. I was here last night. I hope you don't mind if I take a look at the place now that I'm sober."

"Same as any tavern in daylight," he said. He put down his rag and looked at my face.

"I worked the door last night. I don't remember you. And I don't forget a face."

"I don't know," I said. "I was dressed pretty different. But do you remember two big women that were here? Very flashy. We had a drink together."

"Do you know their names?"

"Angela and Marsha." His face changed expression a couple of times and he studied my face like I was a different person.

"Those two," he finally said. "Hard to forget, right? They're here all the time. At least when there's a good DJ."

"You wouldn't know how to get a message to them would you?"

"I might. You know that Angela gives me her number everytime they come in. I can't count how many times. You'd think she'd figure out by now that I'm not interested."

"They do seem to have boundary issues."

We both laughed at that. He didn't have a clue how far they crossed the line. When I found them I was going to let them know they can't just transform people for kicks, even if this was turning into a totally unique experience.

"Can you call her for me?" I asked.

"You can call her yourself," he said. "Last night's love note is in the dustpan."

I followed him to a long handle dustpan propped against the bar. He emptied it into a tall trash basket. There was a slip of paper with the dirt and dust. He shook it clean and handed it to me.

The handwritten scrap had a lipstick kiss above a phone number and the words call me. It was signed with a capital A in a circle like an anarchy symbol.

"If you reach her, please tell her Jeremy gave it to you. Maybe then she'll leave me alone."

"Thanks so much, I hope they pick up" I said. "Just in case, if you see her or Marsha, tell them Randall is going to find them."

"Who's Randall?"

"Yesterday I was."

I left to meet Louise. Outside her building I found a conspicuous spot on the sidewalk. More than one stranger gave me the eye as they passed. Finally, I saw her coming down the street. I let the macramé vest slip down my shoulders as I turned away from her. I stuck out a hip in my best imitation of a working girl. Louise wasn't getting in the building without pushing past me. She closed the distance and as expected, she was direct.

"You're blocking my door, lady."

I turned around to face her.

"You must be Louise."

"Yeah," she said. "Who are you?"

"You can call me..." I paused for effect then whispered, "Miranda."

"Oh my God, Randy is that you?" She took a step away. "That makeup is incredible. And where did you find fake breasts? Those tits look real."

"They are," I said. I took a quick look up and down the block then grabbed the hem of my shirt and flashed her so she could see my naked breasts.

"What the ever loving fuck. Your voice, your tits. Where's Randy? Who are you?"

"I knew you wouldn't believe it," I said. "Let's go inside real quick before I get picked up for street walking."

"But, but…"

"Come on. Let's just go in. I have so much to tell you."

For a moment I didn't think she was going to let me come inside to her place. She wasn't sure who I was. She just kept looking at me and staring down at my hips and butt, then back to my face.

"It kind of is you," she said. "Is this like an AR trick? Some kind of app?"

"I'll tell you inside. But it really is me, Miranda."

Louise unlocked the door. We went up to her apartment and I plopped down on the couch. It felt like I had been going ninety miles an hour all day. And there was plenty more to come. Louise sat at the other end of the couch.

"I'm going to tell you what happened," I said. "You won't believe it but, here I am, so you have to."

I started with meeting Marsha and Angela and then everything since I woke up. Well, I left out my time in the tub but couldn't resist telling her all about William's piercings. Louise was shocked that I went all the way and had a million questions. Before long we were giggling about him. She sat beside me on the couch and without even thinking about it, we were holding hands while we laughed.

"Oh Em effing Gee," she said. "Randy is Miranda. It's incredible."

"Yeah, for a limited time, thanks to science."

"Stand up and turn around," she said.

I did a slow turn in front of her so she could see the full picture.

"Don't bite your lip," she said. I didn't realize I was.

"Do I pass?"

"Pass? Randy, if I had that body I'd be married to a Duke or something. You're hot. Even without that slutty get-up you'd stop traffic."

"I'll have to live with that. Two days, max. Maybe less. That's why I decided to go for it with William. This whole thing is like a one time chance."

"I still can't believe you did it with the clerk."

"They're not a clerk exactly. It was kind of like a service call, I guess. To make sure everything was in good order. And we used a condom."

"So, it's not just the boobs? Like between your legs?" Louise trailed off.

"I'll show you mine if you show me yours."

I said it without thinking. It was the sort of childish thing I would have said to her if we were drunk. Flirting that we pretended was just kidding. Nevertheless, I had just asked my best friend to get naked for me.

The sudden silence gave me time to wonder if she had been waiting a long time for me to ask that. And wonder why I could never ask her as a man.

Louise stood up on the couch, wobbling but holding her balance on the cushions. She pointed at me.

"You're not Randy. Randy doesn't make indecent proposals." She jumped off and circled around me at a distance. She wagged her finger like a prosecutor in a courtroom drama.

"Just who are you, Ms. Sexy Miranda? And where are you hiding Randall?"

"Stop it," I said. "Here. I'll give you a peek." I slid down my leggings to below my knees. My lifted skirt exposed the naked swell and folds off my female body. I wasn't self-conscious. In fact I felt a warm glow of pride, sharing with the one person in the world I trusted completely. Louise turned her head one way and another, convincing herself of what she was seeing.

"Damn my eyes," she said.

"Your turn," I told her. It came out sounding more commanding than I wanted. Louise looked me in the eye. A wide grin broke slowly across her face. I dropped my skirt flap and crossed my arms, giving her all my attention.

Louise untucked her shirt from her blue jeans with a tug on each side of her hips. The shirt tails separated as she undid the bottom buttons. She stopped when she reached the buckle of her jeans.

"Check this out'" she said. She unzipped her pants to show off her underwear. Her panties were decorated with a kawaii neko cat pattern.

"Very nice." I laughed.

She pulled the panty front way down.

"Untrimmed," she said

I saw the cute curls that grew over her sex. We smiled at each other and we both blushed. We stood there like chibi anime girls. I curtsied with my skirt and pulled up my underwear. She shook her hips like a belly dancer. And then we hugged. Long and hard as if it would last forever.

"I'm so relaxed right now," I sighed.

"That makes total sense," she said.

"What do you mean?"

"Randy, this is the woman in you. This is your true soul."

I broke our embrace. It made me uncomfortable when she challenged my masculinity. She didn't let up though.

"As long as we've been friends, you've been awkward. You're always uncomfortable, even when things are going your way. You never have the nerve to kiss me and we've both wanted that. Am I right? The only time I've ever seen you look relaxed, really enjoying yourself, was when I got you in a dress. You may have been drunk, but you were happy."

"But," I objected. "This is a temporary thing. I was dosed."

"Look at the way you're holding yourself, though. A lot of guys would be in a total panic right now. You may not be the Miranda I expected, but you are a natural in that body."

"It does feel nice," I admitted. "I feel awake, connected."

"And horny?"

"Yes... I don't know. William was like an experiment."

"Rationalize it how you want. You've been a woman for half a day. The first thing you did was fuck the hired help."

"Don't be so crude. I would have come right over if you didn't have to work a shift. You know that." I took her hand. "Do you want to explore?"

"Every inch," she said.

My heart was pounding. I wanted to kiss her. We did kiss. We let our lips touch for an instant. Then I kissed her again, longer.

"I like this," I told her.

"Maybe we shouldn't be standing," she said. "Lie down and let me see everything."

Louise led me to her bedroom. The curtains facing the street were closed. The bed covers were still tousled from the night before. She threw some clothes into a corner. Then she backed me up against the mattress, and lifted my shirt up over my head.

"Wow. Did you order them this size? How's your back?"

She touched my chest, squeezing gently with one hand and running her palm under my curves with the other. She gave a firm squeeze with both hands and let go.

"On the bed, bottoms off," she said.

I scooted all the way out of my leggings and panties. The skirt dropped to the floor. Then I flopped onto Louise's mattress and rolled over on my belly.

"Bottoms up, huh?" Louise smacked my butt. "Look at that ripple."

"Stop it," I said.

She sat on the edge of the bed next to me.

"This is so cool." She touched my butt cheeks again, but this time it was a caress. From the tops of my thighs she traced around to my widened hips. She applied pressure up along my spine and rubbed my shoulders. It felt so good to be touched. I've never had a full massage, but I can see the attraction. Louise's hands felt luxurious. She raised my arm and ran a finger across my armpit. It should have tickled, but I was too comfortable with her touch.

"Be a good girl and roll over," she said. "Stop hiding the good bits."

I did what I was told. I propped a pillow under my head and spread my arms and legs out. On my back, my breasts made mounds that rolled to either side. The nipples seemed to float in the middle like lily pads.

"Unbelievable," whispered Louise. She leaned over and blew a raspberry on my belly before buying her face in my boobs and pushing them together.

"Mmmm," she said before sitting again. "I always wanted the jello bowl kind. I'm stuck with these dainty ones. They're cute but I can't do tricks with them. OK. Knees apart."

"Yes doctor," I said. I lifted my knees and moved my feet a little farther apart. Louise circled around me. When she had had a good view, I let my knees fall to the side.

Louise could slap my butt or mess with my breasts and it was just more fooling around. She never thought twice about being in my space. Now, she asked before coming closer.

"Can I touch you there?" She wasn't play-acting an examining doctor anymore. She was intimate, appreciative. I wanted her to. I trusted her.

"Go ahead. Do whatever you want."

She settled between my legs and ran her fingers along the edge of my soft outer lips. Then she drew down between them using only enough pressure to separate them slightly. She rolled her fingers in the protruding folds of my inner lips.

"Like beautiful coral," she said and leaned in to kiss me. I was wet where she kissed.

"So fresh," she said. Her next kiss found my clit. I surprised myself with a little cry. It was so sensitive.

"Miranda likes?"

"It's too nice," I said.

"It gets better," she said. Her next kiss was a lick. Then there were small flicks. Each one stole my breath.

"Oh," was all I could say. I wanted to touch her. She had on too many clothes. I wriggled away.

"If we're going to do this, you get undressed too."

"OK, Miranda."

She pulled her shirt over her head and unhooked a cute purple lace bra. She tossed them aside. Then she buried her head to lick me again. I heard her shoes kicking off. She slid out of her pants without taking her lips off of me. I didn't want her racing me to an orgasm. I wanted her next to me.

"Hug me again," I said. She crawled up beside me on the bed. There we were, two best friends. Two women. Naked. Our arms and legs intertwined. We kissed. I was overwhelmed with my feelings for her.

"You know I've always loved you," I said.

"And I love you, Randy." She moved her hand back to my sex. "You can touch me too, you know."

She didn't have to ask me twice. We explored every inch of each other's bodies. Breathed each other's scents. I made her pulse race as fast as mine. Now Louise slowed me down. She's so high energy I always thought she'd be crazy in bed. But she was so caring. Her touch was uninhibited but never forceful or selfish. Even as the feelings got more intense, I felt supported. William and I had fucked. Louise and I made love.

Our bodies were similar but different. Being a man was a memory. Thoughts of our late nights when I was drunk and wearing her clothes flashed by in little bursts between the peaks of bliss. I stroked her hair and kissed her fingers and ears and sighed a hundred times. A distant voice inside me asked "Who is Randy?" And another voice, a woman's voice, corrected the first. "Who was Randy?" I didn't have answers. I didn't want thoughts. I just wanted this time with Louise to last forever.

We ended up with our legs scissored. Grinding against one another, hands linked together, pulling. My free hand hugging her leg. We were both loud and writhing. After so many of my own peaks, I focused on Louise. Thoughts of my own pleasure faded. Gentleness fell away. I wanted her to come. I worked my pubic bone against hers as only two women can. She gasped, and spasmed and then had to push me away. "Oh, God. That was it. No more."
I spun around to rest my head by hers and we pulled a cover over us. We were sweaty and happy. Louise was glowing. I think I was crying.

# Hanging out in alleys

"Are you really going to put those slut clothes back on? I can find you something else."

I was getting dressed after our long post-sex cuddle. I might have drifted off to sleep if Parker hadn't popped back up in my thoughts. This was the end of my tenure with D&H, but I knew his vile behavior would continue long after I was gone if someone didn't shake him up.

"I know it's tacky and I know you're dying to dress me, but I need to put myself on display if I'm going to mess with Parker. It's not even about the money anymore. He might not budge on that. But honestly, just for revenge it will be worth it to expose his harassment."

Louise was covering herself with a sheet as she sat up in bed. It was funny how modest she was now that we were talking about serious things.

"But what if the two of you are alone and you get horny?" she asked.

"We obviously got most of it out of your system but what if it kicks in? It could be a side effect."

"Gross. Don't say that."

"But how are you going to manage it? What if he gets aggressive? You could get raped."

"Can we still call your cousin for backup?"

"I don't actually have a cousin from New Jersey." There was that grin I loved. I adored her dimples and her jaw.

"Do you want to cosplay him?" I suggested. I've seen Louise dressed up like warriors and ninjas.

"Sorry, I don't have a secret pill to make me a strong man."

"I guess not. Probably safer if you stay behind. But I'll check in when I get there. And then if you don't hear from me in half an hour, come and rescue me."

"Still pretty dodgy."

"It's the best I can do. I'm not giving up on this."

Louise sighed and got out of bed. She was adorable standing there naked and alluring when she bent over to grab some clothes off the floor.

"Come into the bathroom," she said. "I'll teach you how the bad girls do their makeup."

"You, do it for me," I said. "It's not like I'm going to make a habit of it."

"Maybe you will," she said and led me by the hand in front of her brightly lit bathroom mirror.

We faced each other while she applied a base layer to my face. Then she did my eyes and added a lot of rouge to my cheeks. She did her own eyes next. It was much more subtle than the heavy shadow she had done on mine. We looked at each other in the mirror and compared.

"Total harlot," she told me.

"Total hottie," I told her.

"Thank you," she smiled. Then she got out a tray of lipsticks.

There were half a dozen shades of red and at least that many other colors not even counting the black and glitter varieties. Louise sorted out a few options and tried a hot fuchsia on herself. She made faces in the mirror and batted her lashes.

"Too obvious for you, I think. He'll get turned on but might get suspicious. You want something earthier."

She handed me a scarlet red tube. I looked at it, like someone had handed me a gun. Something that was familiar but completely alien in my hand.

"You have to be able to do it yourself," Louise said. "What if you need a touch-up?"

I shrugged and took off the cap. I found the thing to push the makeup out farther and smudged a blob on my upper lip. The color was startlingly bright in the mirror. I stopped with the outer edges of my lips still bare.

"I don't know," I said. "Should it be this bright?"

"Hmm, maybe a little too bloody for indoors." Louise handed me a tissue. "Wipe it off."

I wiped and dry-kissed the paper until no more came off. Louise handed me another tube. It was open and there was a beveled edge to the crayon.

"Just draw slowly and follow the line of both lips," she instructed.

I went slowly and felt my way across my pursed lips. The color went on neatly and I looked at what I had done. Below my long lashes and smokey eyes, my mouth was a rich burgundy red. I could imagine the person in the mirror in candlelight, holding a long stemmed glass, making eyes at her date across the table. I looked hot.

"Wow," I said. "I look so grown up."

"If I put you in a dress you'd be absolutely elegant. But with all the skin you're showing in this outfit, he'll want those lips leaving rings around his penis."

"It's wasted on him," I agreed. "But hopefully he'll pay a price if he makes a move."

I was as ready as I'd ever be. I thought about borrowing a purse to take with, because all my stuff was in a shopping bag from the Soma shop. I didn't want to haul it around with me. Then I remembered the slip of paper I got at the bar. I let Louise know that I had to make a call. I got out my phone and dialed the lipstick signed number. It went straight to a recorded message.

"If you're not looking for Angela, you don't know what you're missing. Either way, leave your info after the beep and I will DM you."

I had a lot to say and barely knew where to start.

"This is Randy from the bar last night. What you two did to me was wrong. I really want to know why. I met your friend Michael and you're in the dog house with him too. Call me back and you better have an explanation."

I was trying to sound angry and assertive but the high pitch of my voice just sounded girly and frustrated to my ears. I left my number and hung up.

"Is it really that bad, Miranda-my-Randy?" asked Louise.

"Not really, at least not this part. But I don't want them to know that."

I sat next to her for a last hug before I headed for the warehouse.

When I got there I stood looking for lights in the upper office windows. Parker's window was bright but not any others. I was ready to check in with Louise when I heard a call.

"Psst, hey! Randy!"

I spun around wondering who could be calling me. I mean who would actually recognize me? The voice wasn't familiar. It was coming from the alley that led to our loading dock. A tall handsome black man in a pinstripe suit stepped into view.

"Randy," he said again. I was stopped in my tracks. I didn't know this person, but the longer I looked at them the more familiar they seemed.

"Hello?" I stood there, curious but not walking into any alley with a strange man, not even the one where I worked. I pulled my macramé vest tighter.

"Ooh, aren't you a sight! It's me, Marshall. You know, Marsha."

And then it clicked. The height was right, the shoulders were right, the vibe was right. As exotic and sexy as Marsha had been last night, this person presented as equally suave and sophisticated. Even standing in reach of a couple of dumpsters.

"Is that really you?"

"In the flesh. I was hoping to catch you here. We need to talk."

I walked over to him. Three feet apart in the alley, we stood checking each other out. I let the macramé vest fall open and did a little sarcastic curtsy.

"I hope you like the results," I said. "You might have asked me first."

"That's just it," Marshall said. "We didn't do it."

"What do you mean you didn't do it? It's a little late to tell stories. Look at me!"

"I know, Michael told me. Good Lord he was furious. Randy, I swear on a stack of bibles that we did not dope your drink. Angela and I only had one spare capsule each. We were saving them."

He seemed so earnest, but it couldn't have been the truth.

"Well obviously somebody gave me Soma. And you were the last people I saw before I woke up like this."

"It's too good." Marshall shook his head. "You are one hundred percent a knockout. This is so much better than anything Angela and I have achieved." He folded his arms and rested his chin on his hand while he studied me. "I don't see any tells. Think about it Randy. Were you 110% convinced that we were women?"

"I didn't know. I was pretty drunk. You seemed like women. There were little moments, but yeah, I was mostly certain. For a minute I wondered if you were cross dressing or.... Did Angela get my message? Jeremy gave me her number."

His face brightened.

"You know Jeremy? Probably not though, on the message. Today's new phone day. We switch all the time. Someone's always on our trail."

Maybe that was why she gave it to the door guy over and over. They might really be on the run. I didn't care about that. I just wanted the facts. Marshall took a step closer and looked serious.

"You have to tell Michael it wasn't us. Otherwise we're in deep trouble. He's a darling but it wouldn't be the first time he's threatened to cut us off and throw us to the wolves. This might be the last straw. I swear there's Russian and Israeli agents everywhere."

He brushed at his lapel as if that would somehow protect him from his pursuers. I didn't know if I could believe a word he was saying. Being chased by foreign spies wouldn't be the craziest thing that was happening.

"Michael saw me. That was all the evidence he needed."

"We wouldn't do that. Not usually. But anyway, I didn't come here just to save my own ass. You must be freaking out." He gave me a convincing look of concern, tight lipped and narrow eyed. He waited for me to speak. I wasn't ready to seek comfort from the person who may have started me on this strange path.

"How did you even find me?" I finally asked.

"We had plenty of clues. You told us all about your job and the asshole you work for. Angela is walking through the neighborhood around Mirror Mirror trying to track you down. I decided to stake out your job."

"Well here I am. How do you explain this if you didn't drug me?"

"You must be a proto."

"A what?"

"A proto. When Angela and I were in Germany setting up our network we got to know some of the scientists. Soma wouldn't be possible if they hadn't isolated a gene from people who transition spontaneously. The lab techs called them protos."

"I never heard of such a thing," I said.

"It's incredibly rare. And usually latent. One in a million people will make the switch at puberty, however except for an occasional tabloid story it goes unnoticed by the rest of the world. Normal people are so messed up you would think they'd celebrate. But not in this fucked up world of ours."

"I'm not going through puberty," I said.

"Well that's the thing," said Marshall. "When the scientists were doing their stuff they didn't just use the proto genes. It's a whole hormonal cocktail. Apparently if a person is a latent proto, being in the presence of someone on Soma can be a trigger."

"What are you telling me?" I asked, not certain if I wanted to know.

"It means your body picked up our scent. Angela's perfume must have been suffused with her pheromones. She wore the expensive stuff last night. Or maybe it was my body powder. Who knows? Either one of us could be your benefactor. But we didn't know. Protos are so rare."

I tried to recall how they had smelled that night. It was hopeless. All I could conjure was the noise and the taste of tequila.

"I don't buy it," I said.

"Think about it, for a bit. Have you ever felt the pull to be someone else? All we did was unlock the potential that was already in you."

Marshall couldn't stop ogling me. His gaze traveling up and down my body was not as innocent as Michael's had seemed. It wasn't the predatory look I got from other men on the street either. He made me feel appreciated.

"Look at you. If it was me that did it, I'm proud."

"This is nuts," I said. "So what happens when the Soma or hormones or whatever wears off?"

"I don't know. I'm sure Michael would be very interested to find out. You are a bit of a miracle child."

"I'm not a child," I said, putting my hands on my hips. And those hips were a testament that I was in fact not a child by anyone's definition. Marshall refused to be put off by my annoyance.

"That's a nice cut up you're wearing. It looks like a William original."

I sighed.

"Yes yes. William did this." I flashed back to the changing room; their bored attitude and made up eyes, and those piercings that were anything but boring.

"I have a few of his originals in my closet," said Marshall.

"Never mind that. What am I going to do?"

Marshall looked around the alley and threw the question back at me.

"What were you going to do? You're dressed to kill. Does that mean you're going to go through with that crazy plan of yours?"

"Yeah, kind of."

"Randy, don't you think that's dangerous? He might assault you or worse."

Pretty much what Louise had said.

"I was hoping it wouldn't get that far. I just wanted to catch a video of him harassing me and send it to his boss. Or post it online. Honestly, once I went in I was just going to improvise."

Suddenly I wasn't sure how safe that would be. But there were two of us here. I could recruit Marshall.

"Hey, I think you owe me," I said. "How would you like to help me out with this?"

"What is it you want me to do?" Marshall's lack of hesitation made it clear he was game for anything. He seemed excited by the risk.

"Parker has been all bent out of shape about a surprise inspection rumor. You can barge in on us announcing that you're a D&H official, come to look at the books. Once I get him to make a move on me, I'll give a signal."

"This sounds like all kinds of fun," Marshall said. "Let's strike a blow for the working class."

I laughed a surprisingly cute giggle at that. "I don't know if putting one over on one boss counts as class warfare, but he deserves what he gets."

We talked over the plan for a minute. I called Louise. I gave her Parker's direct number. She would pretend she was calling from D&H and tell him an inspector was coming in an hour. Marshall was big enough to intimidate Parker in the inspector role without having to get physical. He could threaten to fire him.

I filled in Louise. She said she'd come meet us once her end was set up. Marshall messaged Angela. She responded right away and also agreed to meet us.

"Angela says we should go to Mirror Mirror afterwards," Marshall reported.

"Well some sort of celebration will be in order," I said.

"It will be great. Like a double date," Marshall said and clapped his hands.

"Louise won't be satisfied unless she actually meets you two. Has Angela also changed back?"

"No, she couldn't bear waking up with a dick so she already took her last capsule. She's twice as intimidating as a woman anyway. Believe me if she gets here and hears either of us yelling for help, she'll tear the house down."

"Good, You come in with me now and wait outside his office door. If anybody walks by, just act important. No one cares who comes and goes anyway. It shouldn't take me long to corner Parker. When I'm ready I'll shout 'Damn!' That's your signal to rush in."

"Let's do it." He gave me an excited hug like we were old friends.

# Miranda strikes

On top of everything else, I didn't see how the day could get any weirder. I didn't want to ratchet the day into the danger zone, but things were in motion. I let my vest fall open to show off my cleavage. I hiked the skirt a little lower to show off my midriff.

"Miranda, Miranda," I repeated to myself, channeling my alter ego. "Miranda, international spy. Master of disguise. Sexy badass."

I threw back my shoulders and marched to the door. Marshall fell in behind me. We entered through the employee entrance that took us down the corridor and past the nefarious time clock. I looked at the ticking box which had no more power over me. I wouldn't daydream about stuffing gourmet licorice sticks into the slot to jam it ever again.

It was well after five and my department was empty. I knew Parker would be on the second floor working on payroll. If he got Louise's call he wouldn't leave his office for a while. We went upstairs quietly. Light spilled into the dim hall from Parker's open door. I started a video chat with Louise and muted my speaker. She could watch the action on her way to join us. It would all be saved in the cloud for evidence if we needed it. I handed my phone to Marshall. He could record Parker's voice from the hall and hopefully get some incriminating video when I called him in to end the role play.

After a couple of deep breaths, I posed in the doorway. Marshall was just out of sight. Parker had his laptop pushed back to make room for a spool-fed electric adding machine. He tapped away at it. The rest of the desk was covered with printouts of spreadsheets. The stack of employee punch cards were fanned out at his elbow. He had a black pencil and a red pencil. I knew he used the red one to mark out and deduct time when he could find an excuse to change people's hours. I could see a few time cards already had red markings. After a second of watching him work, I rapped on the door frame.

Parker looked up, startled and unsettled. He must have got the word from Louise that trouble was on the way. When he saw me standing there, his expression morphed into a slimy grin. I was definitely not the D&H inspector. He checked me out, up and down.

"Well hello," he said. "Can I help you?"

"Are you Mister Parker?" I asked, trying to feign a tone of uncertainty.

"Yes I am, how can I help you?"

"Well Mister Parker I'm so very sorry to disturb you. I can see you're busy. If I can have a minute of your time though, I want to ask you about one of your people. Randall?"

"You mean Randy?" His grin faded at the corners. I wasn't surprised by the look of distaste at the mention of my name. He didn't know it was me, but he never hid his dislike for me. He didn't care who knew. Fuck this asshole, I thought. I stepped into the light of his office and pretended to look around. I gave him a good view of my profile and enough of my back to see how I filled out the short skirt.

"Yes," I said, facing him again. "I understand that Randy had, I don't know if you would call it a dispute, but words with you. About his hours?"

"We don't dispute hours here ma'am. Everyone gets paid for the work that they do. But please come in. I'm doing payroll right now."

He hit the enter button on his calculator to advance the little roll of paper with a ding. "As you can see I tally and check everything."

I walked to the desk. He kept a visitor's chair on my side but I had never been asked to sit when he called me in. I leaned over the chair and his laptop to look at the papers. I leaned low like I was nearsighted. I had to move my arm over the bottom of my scissored shirt to keep from exposing myself. That pushed up my cleavage. My breasts were right at Parker's eye level. He licked his lips.

"Yes, well," I said, straightening up. "Randy is my brother and he was terribly upset yesterday. He said he was being unfairly docked. He's not one to question authority, but I know he's concerned about covering his last month's rent. Was there some sort of misunderstanding between you two? Maybe I can help clear up any miscommunication." I let the vest slip a little way down my shoulders. "I'm good at listening to both sides of an issue. Is there anything you can tell me about it, Mr Parker?"

"There shouldn't be anything to clear up, ma'am. What did you say your name was?"

"Miranda," I said. I extended my hand, marveling at how delicate my fingers looked. He held me in his grip a little too long, probably imagining how easy it might be to overpower me. I did my best to smile alluringly.

"Believe me, everything here is in order. I'm sorry that Randy had to waste your time. Did he actually send you here to talk to me?"

"Randy didn't send anybody. I'm here out of the kindness of my heart. Are you sure we couldn't go over his numbers for the week?" I ran a hand through my hair. This time I let the shirt ride up to reveal the underside of one breast. Parker leered openly, realizing a trade of hours for sex might be in the air. But he had to be the one to make a move.

"I have his card right here," he said, reaching for the pile. "If you'd like to go over it with me I can explain how the system works."

"Let's do that. I'd like to see how you handle things." I faked a little laugh and sat down opposite him. He fanned out the cards and quickly found mine. I could see it was already full of red marks. Oh, I was going to enjoy this.

Parker barely looked at the card. He waved me around to his side of the desk.

"You'll see better if you come over here while I go through the numbers."

I pouted my lips a little bit. I was glad that Louise had done my makeup. I shook my mane of hair like I was casting off any reservations as I stood up.

"Why don't you show me. I'm sure you can make it all make sense."

On Parker's side of the desk I was close enough to smell his stale sweat and cheap after-shave. But I leaned closer. William had measured the fabric alteration perfectly. Bending over, my nipples almost but not quite popped out from under the scissor cuts. The excitement of the charade was making them hard. I made sure the vest didn't block his view. The slimeball could barely look at my time card. He squirmed in his chair. It must have taken effort for him not to grab me right there. I was a stranger after all and he didn't know how I'd react. I'm sure he wouldn't have held back with one of the women from the shop.

I pretended to be surprised by my show of flesh. Feigning modesty I pulled the material taut, as if the pressure would push my nipples flat. It just drew attention to them. After a little jiggle of embarrassment, I pulled the macramé across like a curtain for intermission.

"It looks like Randy had a full schedule this week," I said, directing him back to my hours.

"You see these marks here and here, Miranda? Unfortunately Randy wasn't at his station when I checked the floor. I can't actually pay people for the work that they don't do."

"Yes Randy mentioned those," I said. "He said he was ahead on his baskets and helping the guys on the dock bring in some stock."

"You know how it is to be a manager." Parker raised an eyebrow as if he was the injured party deserving sympathy. "If you believe everything that everyone says then no work really gets done. A manager has to be hard."

Well there was an opportunity. I nestled in a little bit closer.

"Are you hard Mister Parker?" I asked. I could guess the true answer to my question.

"In the right circumstances I can actually be a softie," he said. Parker was ready to negotiate. But I wasn't going to pay the price he wanted. I hoped Marshall was picking all this up on my phone.

"That's sweet," I said. "I can be a softie too. You might find out how soft If we work this out."

"I'm not sure what I can do for Randy. What did *you* have in mind?"

"I was hoping we could discuss it over a drink down at the corner."

Parker looked at the clock on the wall and frowned. I knew that wasn't going to happen. Louise had played her part. Parker was in a time crunch. He was expecting to be interrupted at any time.

"Unfortunately I have a meeting here this evening. Not right away, though. There might be something we can do now to set things straight. It's funny how easily these things can get resolved."

"How does that happen?" I said as if I didn't know. I had to get him to say it.

"Let's get to know each other a little better. Maybe you can change my mind about what gets sent to payroll."

I licked my lips.

"Randy and I only want what's right."

Parker stood. He wasn't an inch taller than me, but he tried to make himself seem bigger than he was. He placed his hand low on my back, clearly intending to stroke my behind if I didn't resist. I fought the urge to push his arm away.

"We're both adults," he said. "No reason we can't come to an understanding by burning off a little steam. Would you like to relieve some stress?"

That's when his hand went south. It was the second time that day I had a man touching my curves. His touch was so very different from William's. Parker gripped my ass like he was picking up a basketball. I hated it but some part of me responded. Roleplaying a slinky hot chick was sending my body signals. I could feel the heat that I had brought to the room. My brain and my nethers were not on the same page. I took a step around the desk to get out of his clutches. To Parker that was an invitation. He followed me, assuming I was heading toward the couch. He didn't let me get that far. As soon as he had room to maneuver he was right up behind me. His hands wrapped around my waist before I could retreat. I could feel his dick through my skirt.

"I may be a hard boss," he growled. "But even I can return a favor. This meeting is going to be a pain in the ass." He pushed against me. "A little pre-game action will leave me in a generous frame of mind. I could log your Randall all of his hours."

He started grinding. I was appalled. I did not like the feel of his business. I did not like the way he found the groove between my cheeks right through the skirt. But my hips pushed back against him. Michael had warned me about unplanned responses. Here they were.

I needed to control myself, but I wasn't ready to break character yet. Parker started to dry hump me, making no more pretense of discussion. He was going to have his way with me. Both hands moved to my breasts and started to squeeze. I was about to call for Marshall when Parker let go and stepped ahead of me.

"Why don't we get comfortable on the couch?" he said.

"After you," I told him. I placed myself between him and the door to block any accidental view of Marshall. The couch was safe, it faced away from the hall. Once Parker was seated I saw Marshall walk past waving my phone and giving me the thumbs up. He was getting it all. Now I needed to figure out my exit.

Parker was patting the cushion beside him.

"Lose the sweater and get over here," he said and unzipped his polyester trousers. His junk fell out through the fly of his boxers. He was hard and pointing like a dart. He took it in his hand and gave it a couple of quick strokes.

"There's plenty of room to stretch out," he said. "Unless you'd rather kneel."

He didn't see the horror on my face because he couldn't look away from my tits. My sense of decency overpowered whatever signals my altered chemistry was sending out. Parker was repulsive.

"Take off your top. I want to slap those melons around before you suck me off."

"Damn!" I said.

On cue Marshall burst into the room. He was holding my phone as if he was in the middle of a conversation. I knew he was capturing a good shot of Parker exposing himself as he made his entrance. He pointed the lens right at Parker's crotch.

"I'll call you back," he said into the phone and cast a wink in my direction. He thumbed the stop button and dropped the phone into his suit pocket.

"Harlan Parker? The hell is going on here? I can't believe what I heard coming down the hall."

"Who the fuck are you?" stammered Parker.

"I'm Kensington Marshall from D&H," he boomed.

I pulled the macramé vest across my chest and backed away toward the desk.

"Are you his boss? I came here to confront him about falsifying people's hours," I said. "He's not paying them for the time that they work. When I called him out he propositioned me."

"She's lying!" Parker was off the couch and fastening his pants.

"Your dick was hanging out, sir!" said Marshall. "Nevermind the accounting problems I came here to look into."

"I wasn't expecting you for an hour," Parker stammered. "This was my own personal time. This is none of your business."

"He was intimidating me," I cut in. "Demanding sexual favors just to give my brother the hours he actually worked."

"This bitch was begging me for it," he said to Marshall as if it was the most obvious thing in the world. Surely another man would understand.

"I'm sorry, Mr Parker." Marshall waved his hand. "I can see exactly what's going on here. I don't need to look at your books to know what has to be done. You can't walk this back. I demand you tender your resignation right now. Am I understood?"

"You can't force me to resign and you can't fire me," Parker spat out. "I'm not a D&H employee." His voice went up a register as he spoke. Marshall turned up the heat.

"You will step down and don't think that Pack-It will just re-assign you. You'll be lucky t stay out of court."

Parker was realizing this wasn't going to end well. Marshall stepped into his personal space and crossed his arms. He was cool as a cucumber and solid as a rock. This was better than I had hoped for.

"Come now, if you don't resign D&H will insist you be fired for cause. Pack-It will listen to their biggest client. If it comes to that, they'll have to notify the state's attorney's office. What I walked in on is criminal abuse of your position. You're done. Now write that letter."

"Jesus fucking Christ," Parker said. He flushed a deep red. I don't think I've ever seen such fury up close. I wouldn't give him any quarter. The feeling of his body against mine clung to me like a disease. I felt I'd been pawed by a dangerous predator.

"You are the scum of the earth," I told him right up in his face. "I don't even care what you do about Randall's paycheck. He'll be thrilled just knowing you're gone."

Marshall was relishing his role as a corporate somebody.

"Oh no ma'am, don't worry about a thing. Anyone that has been shortchanged will be compensated. It was good of you to risk speaking out. Maybe we can get you a spot in the home office, away from this drudgery."

I smiled at that.

"Oh, I don't work here. I'm here for my brother."

Parker had his laptop open and was typing. I walked around behind him to see what he wrote.

*To whom it may concern, as of today's date I resign my position as operations manager for the D&H division of Pack-it Industries.*

*Harlan Parker*

Marshall gave an audible shrug when he read the words.

"I want you to cc HR at D&H." He looked at me and asked "On whose behalf did you make this visit?"

"His name is Randall, you can see his time card right there." I gave Marshall a sweet smile. I wasn't sure what we could accomplish, but I was willing to keep up the act and see what Marshall had in mind. The resignation bit was already more than I had imagined.

"Fix these hours before you hit send." Marshall pushed the card at him. "You leave the paperwork with me. Since you are cooperating, I will leave your advances against this young woman out of the report I turn in."

Parker was deflated; it looked like all the fight was out of him as he complied with our demands. I realized I had no idea about his circumstances. Would he be desperate in the morning and try to take back his notice? He would discover that nobody knew who Marshall was. He might try tracking us down. I had to make him think he shouldn't risk it.

"If he backtracks I can get others to corroborate. Randy told me about a woman named Cheryl. Also Annie and Adija. A bunch of women he took advantage of. If you challenge this you are going to have a stream of me-to's to fight."

I couldn't resist throwing back my shoulders and letting the vest slip to give him one last look at my body. I felt powerful in my femininity and Parker had zero claim to it.

Marshall got in the last word.

"I'll have somebody pack your personal effects and that tacky poster. You don't need to take anything with you now."

Parker tried to say something. His jaw flapped but no words came out. He looked back and forth at the both of us before getting up and leaving. When we heard him going down the stairs we both collapsed on the couch. For a minute we just sat and listened. Once it was clear that he wasn't coming back we smiled at each other.

"We did good," Marshall said.

"You were amazing."

"You're pretty badass yourself. It took guts to do what you did."

"I was just going to get the evidence and run. I never dreamed he'd resign like that."

"Let's make sure," said Marshall. We looked at the laptop on the desk. The email window was still open. We double-checked the outbox to confirm that the message had really gone to both companies. Marshall started poking around on the screen, clicking folders. He was digging through directories, clucking his tongue while he looked for something.

"I'm sure this is company property and he shouldn't be using it for personal storage. But a man like him is going to be hiding *something* here that he shouldn't be."

"I shudder to think," I said.

"Aha, there it is. Take a look." He had found a cache of pictures buried in a subfolder. Marshall previewed them in a grid of thumbnails. "Recognize anyone?"

I saw pictures of women taken in that same office. Some were my coworkers, some must have worked there before my time. Not all of them were dressed. Everything was shot from a similar angle. Parker must have set up the laptop to take pictures whenever he had one of his private meetings with the women he harassed.

"This will get him fired for real," I said. "I can't believe all the days I came to work knowing what a shit he was. And everybody just put up with it."

"People are afraid to push back," said Marshall.

"Walking around like this, this morning, I could feel the eyes on me. Parker's not the only one out there."

"True, but we're both guys, and we're not like that. Are we?"

It was a strange question considering Marsha was very much a woman when I met her and I wouldn't be standing next to them if I wasn't very much a woman at the moment.

"My head is spinning," was all I could answer.

Marshall wrapped an arm around me.

"You don't have to answer the big questions right away, Miranda. Just enjoy this little victory."

We zipped up the incriminating folder and sent it to the same addresses as the resignation. We cc'd a couple of other names from his contacts that I recognized as management. I didn't hesitate at all. It felt like I was leaving a legacy behind and hopefully a better workplace for future employees.

# Victory lap

Back out on the street Louise was just coming around the corner from the nearest bus stop. On the opposite side of the intersection we were surprised to see Angela a half block away. Her daytime attire was a summery sleeveless dress. Apparently she had run into Parker on his way out. They looked to be having an earnest discussion. We couldn't hear them, but Angela was nodding and touching his arm as if in sympathy. She looked our way and waved when she saw us. Before Parker could turn around she wrapped an arm over his shoulder and led him away. She was taller so he hurried to keep up while he went on with his story. I could only imagine what he was telling her.

Louise stopped to see what we were looking at before she joined us.

"Is that your boss over there?" she asked.

"He's not anybody's boss anymore," I said. "This is Marshall and that's Angela down the street. Apparently we just missed her. We don't know how she got a hold of Parker."

Louise kissed me on the lips and extended her hand to Marshall.

"So you were a woman when Miranda met you?"

"I am a woman," Marshall answered. "I happen to be in my birth body at the moment. Soma lets me slip in and out as needed."

"Well you're no slouch. Nice to meet you."

Marshall looked down at himself. "It's dashing and all, but not the realest me."

"It's incredible that you have a choice," said Louise. I could tell she was imagining him as a woman. I had seen her look at me that way so many times.

"I like to switch," said Marshall. "Angela hates changing back. She keeps asking me to knock her up so she can stay as she is. I'm not ready for kids though."

As much as I wanted to resent them for my strange circumstances, I couldn't help liking Angela and Marsha/Marshall. If all that stuff about protos was true then I was just a freak of nature. It wasn't their fault. Maybe. I wouldn't mind calling them my friends and I definitely wouldn't want to call them my enemies.

"I think you'd make a great dad, or mom," I told him.

Marshall shrugged and straightened his suit coat.

"I'm sorry I can't introduce you to Angela just yet," he said to Louise. "But I'm sure she'll turn up. Why don't we all head to Mirror Mirror and get to know one another."

I called a ride. We ended up at the same table as the night before. It was still early, and I wasn't ready for any more tequila. Marshall ordered a sparkling wine for everybody, the closest thing they had to Champagne.

"What should we toast to?" I asked.

"To Miranda," Louise said.

"To Marsha and Angela," I said.

"To Soma," said Marshall.

We clinked classes and began chatting. It was no surprise that Marshall had a lot of interesting stories to tell. We let him entertain us while Louise and I played footsie under the table.

I sipped and enjoyed the feel of the bubbles. I marveled at the traces of lipstick on the glass. All felt good with the world except for one small detail. I had no idea what was going to happen to me over the next couple of days. I wasn't sure what I wanted to happen to me. School was coming up. It wouldn't matter what body I finished my classes in. I was already registered. If anyone noticed me on campus, I wouldn't be the first student to have changed genders in one manner or another. No one cared enough about me to pry. After that anything was possible.

While I thought it through, Angela made her entrance. The outside door swung open. She was haloed by the bright light behind her. She looked around, blew a kiss at Jeremy who was at his spot by the entrance, and made a beeline for us.

"What a piece of work!" she said, taking a seat on Marshall's right.

"What were you doing with him?" I asked.

"He was racing past me down the sidewalk. Mad as hell. I wasn't certain who it was but if it looks like an asshole, walks like an asshole, smells like an asshole, I figured it was probably your boss. So I played the hunch. Before he got past me, I asked 'Is everything okay dear?' He whipped around like he was going to throw a punch at me but when he saw this beautiful face he froze in his tracks. It didn't take ten seconds for him to start complaining about his miserable life. And not a minute more than that before he started putting the moves on me. I took him to a dive bar I know. One dark enough that he wouldn't see me drop a cap of Soma in his beer."

"Oh my god," Louise and I squeaked in unison.

"Jinx," giggled Louise. We did a quick pinky shake. "I can't believe you did that."

"And they want me to believe they didn't dose my drink," I said.

"Wait," said Marshall. "I thought you already took your last capsule."

Angela smiled and batted her eyes.

"Sweetheart, the one I gave him was yours."

"Why you unscrupulous tramp," said Marshall. "How could you do that to me?"

"It's OK." She waved away his concerns. "Michael will hook us up. He always comes around."

"That he does."

"Now where's my drink? I need to wash away the taste of that schlub."

I ordered another round. While Louise questioned our new friends, digging for gossip, my mind wandered. I wondered about the status of the Soma project. Was it an open secret? If I did switch back soon would they take me as a customer? I admitted to myself that I might want to do this again. Then again, what if I never changed? Was I leaving my true self behind?

"Penny for your thoughts," Marshall said.

"Just thinking about this proto stuff."

"Are you OK with the new you if it sticks?"

"I think she's perfect as Miranda," said Louise.

"Let the lady think," said Marshall.

"Now that I've lived a whole day of it," I said, "if I could go back and forth I might. After today I don't think I'll ever be the same person no matter what's between my legs."

"There is always the pregnancy option," Marshall reminded me. "If you want to leave Randy behind, that is."

"Wait. what?" said Louise. "I still don't get that part."

I had left it out when I was telling her what I learned from Michael.

"According to the case studies, if you get pregnant while using Soma there are hormonal changes that make the transition permanent."

Louise took my hand.

"And who would the father be, Miranda? Would you just let the clerk do it?"

Marshall laughed.

"William would never agree to that. They avoid paternity at all costs."

"They don't have a version of Soma that would let me be a man for a couple of days, do they? I'd make the switch long enough to knock this one up." Louise kissed my cheek.

"Will you stop planning my life for me?"

"Not a chance, babe."

We locked lips and I don't think we came up for air until Angela was on her second glass.

In what weird world would I be able to have Louise's baby? I wondered. But my thoughts were interrupted when a voice boomed out, "Put your hands where I can see them!"

# Most Odd

We all turned toward the sound of the voice. A tall, broad shouldered man in a trench coat stood between us and the door. His complexion was olive and his square jaw had a five o'clock shadow that blended seamlessly into the fade on his temples. It all grew into a gelled flip of black hair that sat like a confection atop his head. His full lips were twisted into a scowl. He clearly wasn't here to make friends, but something about him was agreeable to my eye.

"Put your hands where I can see them," he repeated. "I'm taking you into custody."

"I didn't do anything illegal," I squawked. I had visions of Parker making a statement to the police.

"They're not here for you," said Angela. She sipped her wine.

"Not at all," said Marshall. "We're the bigger fish."

He sat up tall to confront the stranger. Angela put her hand over his.

"You have no authority here."

"Who is he?" asked Louise.

"He's with Most Odd," said Angela.

"That's Mossad," said the agent.

"The Israeli secret police!" said Louise. It was her turn to squawk.

"These two are wanted for trafficking dangerous pharmaceuticals, and they're not slipping through my fingers this time."

The drinks were going to my head, and I was still flying on the excitement of putting one over on Parker. I downed the rest of my glass and crossed my arms under my bosom. "Show me your badge,"

I demanded. Louise gripped my arm. I bet she couldn't believe I was going to get in this guy's face. "I think he's lying."

"Careful Miranda," said Marshall. "You don't have experience dealing with these twerps."

"Come on, ID," I said.

Louise grabbed her purse. "I'm streaming this live to my followers," she said. "He can't do anything with the whole world watching." She looked the agent in the eye. "You guys are supposed to stay anonymous, right?"

Before she could pull her phone out the man from Mossad snatched Louise's purse from her hand and tossed it to the other end of the table. "I think you all better chill out," he said. He pulled back his suit coat to reveal a gun tucked in his slacks.

"He's got a pistol!" said Angela, loud enough to carry through the club.

"How many inches?" called the bartender.

"If you're trying to make me jealous it's not working," chimed in Jeremy the doorman.

"Guys, I'm serious," said Angela.

"Looks like we have to go," Marshall said to me. "Do us a solid and call the swap shop, will you?"

"But he's armed," I said.

"We'll go quietly," he told the agent. Marshall put his hands up in the surrender position.

"Why quietly?" asked Angela, getting up from her chair.

"You're right," said Marshall. He took a step towards the door and started singing.

"*I'm just a poor boy*," he began and launched into the opening of Bohemian Rhapsody. "*He's just a poor boy*," answered Angela.

"Shut up," said the agent. He fell in and stayed two steps behind Marshall and Angela. He didn't look back at me and Louise.

Jeremy opened the door to the cool evening air.

"Why did you let him in?" Angela asked.

"I assumed he was one of your fans," Jeremy shrugged.

"Only you, darling. You're my only fan."

The agent pushed Angela forward and out the door where Marshall waited with his arms still in the air.

"We have to do something," I said as the windowless door swung shut, cutting us off from the pair who had started me in this whole adventure.

"Do we?" Louise said. She was carrying her empty glass to the bar. Whenever we go anywhere she tries to save the staff some effort.

"What do you mean? They're in trouble." I sighed following her with my own glass.

"I mean guns?" she said. "Do we really know what we're mixed up in?"

"We at least have to call Michael at the Soma shop. We can do that much."

"You don't have to bus your table," the bartender called. "I'll get that." He was by the door conferring with Jeremy.

Louise retrieved her purse. I got out my phone and found the number for Soma. It rang for a long time before going to voicemail. I wasn't sure what I should leave on a recording.

"This is about Marsha and Angela," I said. "They're in the middle of something, could you call me?"

We joined the two guys at the door. I asked Jeremy "Did you ever see that guy before?"

"I'm pretty sure not. I try not to get mixed up in Angela's mischief. Kind of hot, though."

Part of me agreed. He was an eyeful, but this wasn't the time for that. I needed to get a handle on the unfamiliar messages that this body could send me. The bartender twiddled the damp rag tucked in his belt.

"Did that guy actually have a weapon? I never know how to read those two."

"Yes he did," said Louise.

"Sorry," he said. "If I had realized I could have hit the panic button."

"I don't know if they would have wanted to add cops to the mix," said Jeremy.

"Standard procedure," the bartender shrugged.

"Did *you* ever see the guy before?" I asked.

"Nope. Another guy was asking about them earlier in the week though. I didn't tell him anything but I took his card. In fact I totally forgot about it. Don't tell them?"

He seemed kind of lackadaisical about forgetting what might have been important. Then again, he's not anybody's secretary. Everyone seemed pretty relaxed about my two new friends being nabbed by some kind of spy.

"Can I see the card?" I asked.

"Sure."

He went behind the bar and brought back a business card from a caddy next to the register. I didn't recognize the logo, but the agency name was clear. Interpol, it said in block letters. Agent Frank Mirovic, with two numbers. One local and one apparently European.

"Shit," I muttered and handed it to Louise.

"We're in over our heads," she said.

"Keep it if you want," said the bartender before he walked away.

I opened the door to the sidewalk and stepped out with Louise.

"Come back soon," said Jeremy.

# Keeping track

Outside there was no sign of Marshall or Angela. I looked up and down the street. Nothing. But not no one. Of all people, William was standing nearby at a bike rack in front of the next storefront.

"A foreign agent grabbed Marshall and Angela!" I said.

"I saw," they replied in their deadpan way.

They were wearing black bike shorts with the same black dress shoes and shirt they had on at Soma Swap. They looked silly with sheer black socks running halfway up their calves. I had an instant flashback to their nakedness. I shook the image from my head. Stay in the moment, there's so much going on. Behind them on the rack was a retro touring bike with fenders and a chain guard. It was all spray-painted matte black, without a hint of shine or chrome. The only exception were red streamers hanging from the hand grips. Honestly they looked like little floggers.

"The guy had a gun!" said Louise. "Why is no one freaked out about this but me?"

"I'm concerned, not freaked out," I said. "Honestly, the two of them didn't seem that upset."

I brought William up to date with as much as we knew.

"They wanted me to call the shop but no one answered. I don't know what to do next."

"Relax," said William. "I put a tracker on the agent's car. Let me transfer the app to you. Is your Bluetooth on?"

"Wait, what do you want us to do? Can't you track them? Oh, this is Louise by the way. Louise, this is William."

She looked William up and down.

"That's the guy? With the metal in his junk?" She circled her hand in front of her crotch. I flushed red. I didn't mean to betray William's privacy. I never imagined Louise would meet them.

"You fucked Miranda?" she asked in a tone somewhere between doubt and admiration.

"Nice to meet you," William said with complete indifference. "I can't follow them, my book group meets tonight. Use the app. It'll show you where they are."

William went back to their bike. As they strapped on a helmet they relinquished one last bit of information. "Oh by the way, Michael is Marla for a few days. If I run into her I will tell her to check the office messages."

William steered the bike into the street and we were on our own.

I launched the phone app and saw a green dot moving slowly in the direction of downtown. "I don't think there's anything we can do while they're moving."

"There isn't," said Louise. "Why don't we go back to my place. Once they stop moving you can leave another message with their people. Then we can make out some more."

"Make out? If what we did was making out, then what would you call *fucking*?" I whispered the word like it was going to somehow get us in trouble. We were standing on a city sidewalk and anybody could be coming around the corner. Being self-conscious was not unusual for me, but I was amused by my own embarrassment. What was exploring my female sexual responses compared to this sudden brush with danger? Our new friends had been abducted and we were clueless.

"I need to know that they'll be okay," I said. "I want to go by the Soma shop, at least. I owe them."

"Owe them for what? You've known them for a day and we don't even really know what crimes they're accused of."

"I kinda trust them. They made me like this. At least I think they did."
The possibility that I was what Marsha had called a proto puzzled me.
Should I have suspected? Does a caterpillar know that someday it will
fly? Louise brought her face close to mine. She looked excited and
expectant.
"You're grateful to them about this?"
"Right now, yeah." Maybe they were pranksters. Maybe they were just
my catalyst. I had felt good all day. It wasn't just the drinks and the
victory over Parker.
Louise hugged me.
"You're the best," she whispered in my ear. I gave her a squeeze. Was
this her fantasy as much as mine? Did she know me better than I know
myself? I had to consider, but we needed to move on from this corner
outside Mirror Mirror. I switched my phone from the tracker screen
where the green dot continued to move away, to a ride-share.
"I hope the shop isn't closed. It's not eight yet."
"You won't be able to rescue them dressed like that. At least come over
and change. We'll get Miranda dressed for the case, Miranda."
It seemed like Louise wanted me to herself. I wanted to be with her but
couldn't abandon Angela and Marsha. Still, the urgency of the moment
was fading. With Michael out of the picture, what good would going
to Soma be? I gave in. Why not stay with Louise until there was a clear
course of action. I pocketed my phone and we walked to her nearby
apartment.

# Whose life is it?

In half an hour Louise had me decked out in a double belted red trench coat with a matching wide brimmed hat. It wouldn't be inconspicuous, but it made me feel like a professional. Professional what, I wasn't sure. "It's a good fit," she said. "If you keep the belt tight, it doesn't hide your curves."

I was enjoying playing dress up until we had more information to act on. I saw some pieces in the costume trunk that I wouldn't mind trying on for other occasions. I thought about my looks as I never had before. What would attract the right kind of guy, I thought. That surprised me. I had come so far before finally admitting my love for my best friend. Now I was thinking about being with men.

"Are you sure about the hat, Louise?" I asked.

"Trust me, Miranda. So how about that William for a sperm donor?"

Louise's question broke my mood. I knocked the lid of the trunk closed.

"Would you stop trying to pick me a baby daddy? You don't get to decide my life for me."

I clenched my jaw and my nails dug into my palms as I blew at a strand of hair that had fallen over my face. When it dropped back into the same spot, I growled in frustration.

"Miranda, Randy, please don't be mad." She took a step toward me, but I circled around her.

"You never ask me what I want. You just have big ideas about what I should do. Sometimes I feel like I'm your dress up toy."

"Randy, I want to make you happy."

"Can't you let me figure that out?"

"You've been trying to as long as I've known you."

That stung. If you had asked me the day before, I would have sworn I was happy. A little uncertain about my prospects, sure; but I thought I knew how to play the game of Life. This transformation had made me realize that I wasn't really happy at all. I had just settled for the mediocrity of assigned roles. White male. College educated drudge. Urban apartment dweller. I was drawn to Louise because she was my embodiment of freedom. We loved being together, but I had settled for existing in her shadow.

"Maybe I finally have a clue about myself." I wrapped my arms around her, burying my face in her neck. I was overwhelmed by a feeling of being home. In my body. No, not in a body, but as a woman. I held my one true friend. Louise knocked the spy hat off of me and ran her hands through my hair as she caressed the back of my head.

"If this wears off," I whispered, "can you teach me to be a real woman? To be the female Randy, not some made up character from a cosplay."

"It would be a privilege, lover," said Louise.

The word made me melt. We kissed gently on the lips and rubbed noses. I held her hand as I stepped away.

"I want to do it without Soma. If I can be comfortable as a woman even with man stuff, then I'll know. We can talk about making babies when we're really sure."

Her eyes sparkled with a happiness I had never seen before. Her smile was like a sunrise. The back of her hand brushed my cheek.

"We should check on the dynamic duo. They must be somewhere by now." Louise did care about them. Everything was aligning.

The app showed the path of the green dot. It had circled downtown, made a line north past the Soma shop, and now had circled back into our neighborhood. They must be going back to the bar I thought, but why?

"Louise, what if Mossad guy is coming back to eliminate witnesses?"

"Crap," she said. "Do we need to hide somewhere?" She went to look out the street side window.

"Wait, I've got Angela's number. Let's try it and see who picks up." I checked recent calls and redialed Angela.

She picked up on the first ring.

"Miranda?!" she asked in her grand theatric way.

"Angela, are you OK?"

"We're fine, doll. We're on our way to see you at your friend's place."

"How do you know where we are?"

"William," she sighed. "He keeps track of everybody. Don't trust him, that's all I can say. We'll be there in a minute. Does Louise have any champagne?"

"Tequila," Louise called into my phone.

"Even better, love. Wash some glasses, we're bringing company."

The connection broke and we looked at each other. "I have no idea," I said. Once again things seemed to be happening fast and those two were taking it in stride. Maybe she had dealt with the agent the same way she had dealt with Parker. I wondered if he was a woman yet, or if he needed to sleep first.

"Do you think this place smells like sex?" asked Louise.

"They'll be the first to tell us, I'm sure. But it's fine with me. Don't tell me you're embarrassed."

"Not possible," she giggled and squeezed my breast through the trench coat. "Put your spy hat back on. You want to impress whoever they've got in tow. I'll slice some limes."

I cracked a window just in case there was evidence in the air of our afternoon delight. I was putting loose clothes, including the "William Original" away in the costume trunk when the bell rang. I buzzed them up.

Angela poured through the door arm-in-arm with Marsha. Marshall had transformed again and she was more feminine than ever. She still wore the tailored suit from earlier, but it hung different on her now.

Her face was glowing with health and excitement. I didn't catch any of the little tells that made her gender uncertain when I first met her outside Mirror Mirror. No one would believe she had ever been a man.

"I thought you didn't have any more Soma," I said.

"Everything's changed," said Marsha.

"What a day," said Angela. Then over her shoulder she called "Come on in, Frankie."

The man who stepped into Louise's apartment was golden blonde and dressed like a tennis pro. His arms bulged out of the sleeves of his white v-neck polo shirt. His pants were black polyester, probably with some spandex because they hugged his butt nicely. He wore them well with deck shoes but no socks. He interrupted my taking inventory by extending his hand.

"Frank Mirovic," he said. "Pleased to meet you."

"The Interpol guy," Louise exclaimed.

"Did someone finally look at one of my calling cards?" He laughed, a deep bass chortle. My hand felt delicate in his. He didn't squeeze, but he clasped both hands over mine briefly before letting me go and extending his greeting to Louise.

"He saved our lives," said Marsha.

"You were in no danger. Mossad is nothing," said agent Mirovic.

"Is no one afraid of people with guns?" said Louise as she dragged another chair into the room from the kitchen. Angela had already cozied up on the couch with her shoes off and her knees pulled up under her chin.

"Make yourself at home, why don't you," said Marsha.

"No no, she's fine. Everyone find a seat and tell us what happened."

"Daveed was nothing more than a middleman," said Agent Mirovic with authority. "Alliances changed long before he bumbled his way into your business. He thought he was trying to stop Soma, but what his bosses really wanted was Michael's formulation. He was a day late and a shekel short." He shook his head slowly then looked at each of us in turn as if weighing our reactions to his words.

To me Frank looked like he could use a drink. I wanted him to feel at home. Even if it was Louise's home. I went to the kitchen to get the tray of glasses and limes we had set up. I briefly wished I had a D&H basket to serve, but that life seemed like a fading Polaroid. Maybe we could order pizza.

I thought I caught Frank checking me out as I walked to the kitchen. He seemed amused being surrounded by a gaggle of women full of excited energy.

"It wasn't the gun that bothered me so much as the abandoned warehouse he brought us to," chimed Angela. "There could have been rats."

"Scoot over," said Marsha, plopping down next to her. "Most Odd was frisking us and getting out the cuffs when Frankie came out of the shadows and told him to step away. I'm sure he was going to try torture."

Frank had straddled a straight back chair, crossing his arms over the top. "I had been following him for days. I decided to let him do the work of finding you two. He's crossed my path before. I was sure once I showed my face he'd know who's top dog."

"You really put him in his place," said Marsha.

"I just laid out the facts. He knows I have free reign in the field and my boss has direct lines back to his boss. Nothing was going to happen to you."

"You make us feel so desirable," said Angela. "But we've gotten out of worse scrapes. Remember when we gave you the slip in Ibiza?"

My world felt small and ordinary listening to these people. Louise and I exchanged glances. *Wow*, she mouthed.

"We've been chasing you two for so long," Frank continued, "we decided to make it right and bring you into the fold."

"We have total amnesty!" Marsha and Angela announced together. They looked giddy.

"And he recruited us. The deal was sealed when Frankie gave us a brand new batch of Soma." Marsha made finger guns and pointed at herself. "As you can see it's fast acting."

"There was nothing Daveed could do. Boy was he pissed. Soma will be legal before the new year." Frank shrugged.

I was standing there holding an unopened bottle by the neck. Louise was at my shoulder. I felt silly in my dress up hat. Frank was dressed so casual and he was the real spy in the room. The Mossad agent had been more of the brusque enforcer type.

"Is Daveed the Mossad guy's name?" I asked.

"Yes," said Angela. "And he asked about you."

"What?"

"Yes ma'am. You made quite an impression at Mirror Mirror. I think he likes you."

"She's taken," said Louise.

Is this what it's like to be popular, I wondered. I popped the cork on the tequila and handed the bottle to Frank. He started to raise it to his lips but thought better of it and reached for a glass. Big as he was, he had no problem stretching over the back of the chair to the tray on the coffee table. He was lithe, with that buff manliness I always found intimidating as Randy. It was matched with the sort of dominating personality that comes from confidence, not meanness. I just couldn't relate to that in my nerdy bookish world. But I was seeing men with new eyes. The earnest good nature he exuded seemed right at home in his powerful body.

"Stop checking him out," Louise whispered in my ear.

Frank winked at me and raised his glass. He must know that I was this way because of Soma. It clearly made no difference to him.

Marsha took the bottle from him. She poured two shots and handed one to Angela. "You kids make a great couple," she said. "Even if Randy switches back, I can see you're good for each other." Then she gave me a sideways glance. "But I've seen Daveed in a speedo. He'd make a good breeder if you decide to go the pregnancy route to lock in this look."

"When did you see Daveed in a speedo?" asked Angela.

"I can have secrets. You don't have to know everything."

Louise took the bottle and had a swig without a glass.

"Nobody is going to breed Miranda. If she switches back she can stay that way and still live as a woman. The parts don't matter. I will love her just the same."

Louise was speaking my feelings. Hearing the words made me resolve to be the kind of woman that she would want to keep around; even if that kind of woman ended up back in a man's body.

Frank reached into the pocket of his slacks. He dug out a small bag of pills and tossed it to me. They were tiny black capsules with no markings.

"It's good to have options," he said.

"This is the really magical part," Marsha said. "Along with the amnesty we are going to rep for a new unit. Interpol got Michael's formula before the Israelis. They've perfected it and have big plans to use it on the continent. You see how fine I look? This is the good shit."

"Soma's going to change the world," said Angela.

I looked at the capsules in my hand. They seemed to vibrate. *A new world*, I thought.

"Nobody's using the limes or salt," I said. "Let me show you the right way to drink tequila."

I handed Louise the salt shaker. Before setting up a shot, I opened the costume trunk and tossed the pills inside. *Maybe, maybe not. Save it for a rainy day*. For now, I had conquered my evil boss, come out to my true love, and got dropped into the middle of international intrigue. I was ready to relax and play hostess. It was time for less thinking, more drinking, and a lot of being the woman of my dreams.

# Don't miss out!

Visit the website below and you can sign up to receive emails whenever Penny Flowers publishes a new book. There's no charge and no obligation.

https://books2read.com/r/B-A-RAIQ-CHLEC

Connecting independent readers to independent writers.

# Also by Penny Flowers

**Hobbes Town Crazy**
Margie's Haunted House

**Standalone**
Randy is Miranda A Gender Transformation Caper

# About the Author

Penny Flowers loves telling tales of the unexpected that surprise her readers and characters alike.